Sherwood Anderson

Early Writings

Sherwood Anderson in Chicago, *ca.* 1917

Sherwood Anderson

Early Writings

৯

Edited by

Ray Lewis White

The Kent State University Press

Kent, Ohio, and London, England

© 1989 by The Kent State University Press, Kent, Ohio 44242
All rights reserved
Library of Congress Catalog Card Number 88-13931
ISBN 0-87338-374-5
Manufactured in the United States of America

Library of Congress Cataloging-in-Publication Data

Anderson, Sherwood, 1876-1941.
  [Selections. 1989]
  Sherwood Anderson: early writings / edited by Ray Lewis
    White
    p. cm.
  Bibliography: p.
  ISBN 0-87338-374-5 (alk. paper)
  1. Anderson, Sherwood, 1876-1941—Knowledge—Commerce.
  2. Advertising. I. White, Ray Lewis. II. Title.
  PS3501.N4A6 1989
  813'.52—dc 19

                             88-13931
                                CIP

British Library Cataloging-in-Publication data are available.

In honor of

Walter B. Rideout, James Schevill,
and William A. Sutton

Pioneers in Anderson Country

Contents

Preface

There is only so much truth in the statement that Sherwood Anderson (1876–1941) became a great writer in 1919. True, Anderson had displayed his first genius as an author when, in the winter of 1915–16, in middle age, he had unexpectedly conceived and demonstrated a new way of telling stories about imaginary but true characters in a fictional Ohio small town—stories that were immediately remarkable when collected and published in 1919 as *Winesburg, Ohio* and that were ultimately revolutionary in the development of the modern American short story. For Ernest Hemingway, William Faulkner, John Steinbeck, William Saroyan, Thomas Wolfe, Katherine Anne Porter, Eudora Welty, and Flannery O'Connor, among other writers of their own and newer generations, would learn much from Anderson's inspired discovery of how to limn human character quickly and tellingly, of how to make the epiphanal "moment" the center of artistic literary achievement.

And yet, when *Winesburg, Ohio* appeared in 1919, Sherwood Anderson had long been a published author. He had by then published two novels; and he had written poems, essays, and short stories that had appeared in such innovative periodicals as *Seven Arts, Little Review, Forum, Smart Set, Masses, Poetry,* and *Dial.* Yet almost forgotten is the fact that earlier, before his actual literary emergence just before World War I, Sherwood

Anderson really had, for many years, made his living by writing—actually, since 1900, when he had become an advertising-agency solicitor and copywriter.

Anderson's fortuitous early discovery of the joys of writing had led him to create in the most unpromising forum—in essays on the profession of advertising—the dramatic situations and interesting character presentation necessary to successful fiction. He had later, as a businessman, accepted and won the challenge of writing a short story good enough for publication in *Harper's*. He had become a successful business executive; and then, precipitously, in middle age, he had abandoned his business career for the uncertainties of an artist's life—the uncertainty of money, of survival, of literary inspiration, and of public recognition. And, by 1915–16, conceiving and composing the Winesburg stories, he had found his best way to live and to create and to be as happy as he could be.

I am presenting this first collection of the earliest published writings of Sherwood Anderson because these writings must be preserved and studied and appreciated for what they are—the apprentice work of a serious literary artist. Collected from various periodicals and magazines issued from 1902 into 1916, these essays and stories are part of the personal history of Sherwood Anderson, part of the public history of his nation as it entered the twentieth century, and part of the common cultural history of humanity—a record of what once was thought and known and believed and what may again be discovered and understood and enjoyed.

In presenting this generally forgotten and sometimes obscure material, I have added to the Anderson canon several hitherto unknown essays and stories. I have in notes explained the few historical and cultural allusions unlikely to be commonly remembered. I have woven the essays and stories into the texture of Sherwood Anderson's life as he grew from a dashing young man-about-town to a respectable middle-class husband and father and then to an unconventional, colorful, and fascinating literary figure.

Knowledge and understanding of what Sherwood Anderson wrote first will lead to greater comprehension and appreciation of what Sherwood Anderson wrote as a mature, gifted, and often inspired and inspiring American author.

Acknowledgments

I am thankful to the following individuals for their aid in my work on this book: Charles Harris, William Woodson, Richard Dammers, and Gary Summers of the Department of English, Illinois State University; Helga Whitcomb and Joan Winters of Milner Library, Illinois State University; Hilbert H. Campbell and Charles E. Modlin of Virginia Polytechnic Institute and State University; and Walter B. Rideout of the University of Wisconsin.

Too late for use in preparing this book I learned of one dissertation written about some of Anderson's earliest writings: Karen-Elisabeth Mouscher, "Sherwood Anderson: The Early Advertising Years," Northwestern University, 1986. The interested reader should consult this study of Anderson's literary development.

On behalf of all students of the life and work of Sherwood Anderson, I remember and gratefully acknowledge the generous assistance and friendship of his widow, the late Eleanor Copenhaver Anderson.

R.L.W.

Introduction

The year 1899 was a year of wonders, a veritable annus mirabilis, in business and production. To paraphrase a celebrated epitaph, prosperity left scarcely any of our industries untouched and touched nothing it did not enrich. It would be easy and natural to speak of the twelve months just past as the banner year were we not already confident that the distinction of highest records must presently pass to the year 1900.

Thus did the *New York Times* greet the year 1900, to most Americans the start of the twentieth century, no matter that the new century would officially begin with 1901. And the *Times* had facts to support its pride in the year past and its optimism for the year ahead: in 1899, the United States had exported $1,252,500,000 in agricultural and manufactured goods; grown 2,500,000,000 bushels of corn, 547,000,000 bushels of wheat, and 9,000,000 bales of cotton; and mined 47,250,000 tons of hard coal, 190,000,000 tons of soft coal, and 295,000 tons of iron. The new year of "noughty-nought" should easily eclipse previous economic achievements as the nation began its fourth century—a century of greatness emerged, certainly an "American" century.

And the year 1900 proved the accuracy of the optimists' predictions. In that year, the population of the United States reached 76,094,000, of whom 38,869,000 were male and

37,226,000 were female; of whom 66,901,000 were white and 9,193,000 were non-white; of whom 30,160,000 were urban and 45,835,000 were rural; and of whom 50.5 percent received formal schooling and whose median age was 22.9 years, with life expectancy of 47.3 years. In 1900, there arrived in America 448,572 immigrants; there were 39,673 patent applications filed; there were 214,000 veterans of the recent and successful Spanish-American War; there were at least 1,174,000 businesses; there were 7,129,990,000 pieces of mail to be delivered; and the average annual wage for all workers was $438.00.

Of the almost 46,000,000 rural Americans in 1900, there were 5,752,000 farm owners and renters, 7,000 farm foremen, and 5,115,000 farm laborers to care for the 750,000,000 farm implements, the 13,969,442 horses, the 2,086,027 mules, and the 16,292,360 cows; and each farm laborer earned for his work over the entire year of 1900 an average of $247.00. The typical farmstead in 1900 remained isolated, each farm family living almost self-sufficiently at its compound of house and outbuildings. Electric lighting, running water, indoor plumbing, and refrigeration were unattainable luxuries. Roads to town were unpaved, trips to town by horse-drawn vehicles were difficult and infrequent, and the recent advances in mechanical invention to aid the farmer and the farm wife were only improvisations on earlier machinery, for the American farm of 1900 would continue for many years to lack electrical and gasoline-powered equipment. In the predominantly rural and agricultural America of 1900, when almost every citizen either farmed or was directly dependent upon farmers, when there was money to be made in serving the commercial and social interests of American farmers, one more ambitious young American joined the nation's 12,000 advertising agents and salesmen eager to prosper in the new year and the new century.

Sherwood Anderson arrived in Chicago in the summer of 1900, having just completed in one year the high-school education missed in his youth in the small town of Clyde, in nor-ern Ohio. Having decided, after foreign service in the brief Spanish-American War, that the road to wealth and happiness in his country lay paved with education and hard work, young Anderson, age twenty-three, lived in Springfield, Ohio, to attend the Academy of Wittenberg College in 1899–1900. There, in Springfield, Anderson first came in contact with business and college leaders in his year of studying such subjects as Latin, German, English, geometry, and physics; and there he first came to admire the knowledge and the attitude of the educated people among whom he now lived and wished to live—people who spoke and wrote literately, people who lived as much in the world of ideas as in the world of physical work, people able to use words to give form and expression to their needs and their dreams.

Among other sophisticated individuals to be met and emulated in this one intense and exciting year of formal schooling, amid his studies in fourteen courses, Sherwood Anderson became acquainted with representatives of the several magazines and newspapers published in Springfield; and, upon completing his high-school education in the spring of 1900, Anderson gladly accepted from one of his new Springfield friends an offer of work in publishing—a position in the advertising department of a major magazine, the *Woman's Home Companion*, work that would return him to the great city of Chicago.

For Anderson had lived before in Chicago, that metropolis which attracted ambitious young men from throughout the Midwest—young men who believed that the great city would accept their hard work and their dreams of success and reward them, inevitably, with the money and the happiness that were the expected results of living out the American Dream. Escaping from the Ohio small town of his youth, young Anderson had endured and survived in Chicago from the autumn of 1896 to the spring of 1898, when the war with Spain promised him adventure away from warehouse drudgery in the city that so far had not recognized or rewarded his ambition to become rich and happy.

In Clyde, Ohio, where he lived from 1884 until after his mother's death in 1895, Anderson had known the shame of poverty, of not having a successful father or a cultured mother, and of not having more cultured surroundings than a farm town of 2,500 citizens. To support himself and his brothers and sisters, Anderson had worked in Clyde at selling newspapers, grooming horses, carrying water, painting houses and barns, delivering merchandise, and building bicycles—any work that would ease the poverty that he bitterly remembered enduring from his youth. Yet the even harder physical labor in Chicago warehouses had not brought Anderson wealth or happiness, even though, knowing that he lacked education beyond the eighth grade, he tried energetically in Chicago to combine his warehouse work with night study in business arithmetic.

Now, two years later, armed with the formal education and the social maturity that he had lacked before and with new knowledge of how to live and work with ideas instead of with physical strength alone, a dashing Sherwood Anderson returned in 1900 to Chicago with confidence in himself and his country, with firm expectation that his drive and his education would this time lead to success.

And success did come quickly, for, after only a few months of working in Chicago for the *Woman's Home Companion*, Anderson was invited by another friend from the past year in Springfield, Ohio, to become a solicitor of advertising and a writer of advertising copy for the Frank B. White Company, an agency that specialized in the marketing of advertising in the agricultural newspapers and magazines that served the American farmer and his family in 1900.

As a copywriter for the White agency, Anderson was responsible for producing the concepts and the words that would sell products and services to farmers. Supplementing his boyhood knowledge of farmers and their needs, Anderson learned how to market cures for animal diseases; mechanical equipment for planting, growing, and harvesting crops; seeds and plants that would dependably increase harvest; and devices that promised to lessen the arduous labor of the farmer and his wife. There is every reason to believe that Anderson was successful in copywriting for his manufacturing clients—agricultural interests and others—for the young man had become aware of words and their power to convince and to persuade and to sell. And in the second aspect of his work for the White agency, Anderson, as solicitor, also succeeded, for he was expected to travel as necessary to bring in advertising business from the makers of products and manufactures to be sold to farmers through the agricultural newspapers and magazines. Easily able to solicit sufficient advertising and to write effective advertisements, Anderson was succeeding professionally at last in Chicago and in the world of American business that he had claimed for his home.

And the media that appealed specifically to the American farmer in 1900 were organized and extensive businesses. With over four hundred newspapers and magazines published throughout the nation devoted totally to serving the farm economy, the agricultural press in America had learned how to sell to the American farmer the products of the American manufacturer, such sales implemented by the advertising solicitor and copywriter. Among the farm papers were such national publications as *American Agriculturist, Country Gentleman, Farmer's Guide, Farm and Fireside,* and *Farmer's Tribune;* such regional publications as *Indiana Farmer, Dakota Farmer, Kansas Farmer, Northwest Pacific Farmer,* and *Iowa Homestead;* and such specialized publications as *American Pigeon Keeper, Wool Markets and Sheep, Poultry and Belgian Hare Standard, National Poultry Journal, Dairy and Creamery,* and *American Bee Journal.* Even more localized and specialized were such journals as *Hospodarksi Listy, Deutsche-Amerikanischer Farmer, Pokrokzapader, Der Wanderer, Skandinavisk Farmer Journal, Der Gefluegel Zuechter,* and

Acker und Garten bau Zeitung. Every state and territory had its farm journals; in Chicago alone, over forty agricultural newspapers and magazines were published.

The Frank B. White Company, considering itself a leader among agencies specializing in the writing and selling of advertisements to the American farm press, furthered its position by publishing a trade journal to appeal to all of the other American agencies that specialized in serving the farm press. *Agricultural Advertising,* founded in 1894, was by 1900 an impressive, well-designed, and well-printed monthly magazine, available from the agency for ten cents a copy or one dollar per year. Subtitled *A Monthly Journal Pertaining to Agricultural Newspaper Advertising,* published at the White Company office, 1700–1712 Fisher Building, Chicago, and claiming an eastern office on Nassau Street in New York City, *Agricultural Advertising* described its function thus: "Our one specialty is assisting manufacturers and other business men in selling goods to farmers. We have made a life long study of it. We have succeeded in many cases where the advertiser hardly hoped for success." *Agricultural Advertising* did not, therefore, print advertisements for goods and services that might be sold directly to the farmer; instead, it printed advertisements from the farm journals and newspapers that solicited business from the advertising agencies that hoped to sell products to the farmer.

Although most of the articles in *Agricultural Advertising* dealt with the practical and beneficent business methods by which advertising agencies could most efficiently and profitably write and sell advertising copy, the trade journal tried to entertain its readers with poems, illustrations, essays, clever and witty sayings, and notes about activities among other advertising agencies and their copywriters. The editors of *Agricultural Advertising* did not solicit contributions to their pages, but they were always willing to note talent within the Frank B. White Company and to consider publication of interesting writings by their fellow-workers. Thus, just months after assuming his duties as solicitor and copywriter at the White agency, Sherwood Anderson, at twenty-five, became a published author, for in the February 1902 issue of *Agricultural Advertising* appeared his first professional writing.

1

The Farmer Wears Clothes

Agricultural Advertising 9 (February 1902): 6.

❧ *Some of the* big, general advertisers seem to be grasping the fact that the agricultural press is tucked up close to the hardest reading, best living class of people in the world, the American farmer. Still, there are, as one of our friends remarked a year ago at Milwaukee, "acres of diamonds that have never been worked." [1]

Here on the desk is one of our best 25-cent magazines. A glance through its advertising pages shows several full-page advertisements of ready-made clothing. Now, is it not fair to say that at least one-third of the readers of a magazine of this character are women? I would venture the assertion that one-half of the men who are on their list have all of their clothing made by a tailor, and that there is only a small proportion of the possible buyers remaining that do not live in the country, and could not be reached through the agricultural press.

On the other hand, the farm paper goes to the man who always buys his clothes in the clothing store. Its pages are filled with matter of vital importance to him and his success. It is read by every member of the family, and the hired man. If there are any young fellows about the place, and there always is at least one, he has a girl. On Sunday afternoons he hitches up the best horse in the barn, carefully groomed for the occasion, and drives off down the road in a spotlessly clean buggy. That fellow has dollars in his pocket—very likely a bank account—and down in his heart there is a longing to be just as well dressed when he goes forth to town, or on his weekly mating tours, as any other man.

If a manufacturer can convince this fellow, or his father either, for that matter, that his particular line of clothing is the proper and right thing to wear, it is going to open up a veritable gold mine for that manufacturer. There is one way, and only one way, to do it. That is, by talking to him in the right way, in the best paying advertising mediums on earth—the high-class farm papers.

1. Joseph A. Ford of the periodical *Farm and Fireside*, published at Springfield, Ohio, read his paper "Acres Of Diamonds" before the National Agricultural Press League meeting 1 November 1900 in Milwaukee. In the essay, published in the November 1900 *Agricultural Advertising*, Ford's subject was "in connection with advertising. The diamonds are neglected opportunities lying around at the very doors of the agricultural implement and vehicle manufacturers." Ford had borrowed the title of his composition from Russell Conwell's famous inspirational 1888 sermon *Acres of Diamonds*.

It is likely that Sherwood Anderson gave to the editors of Agricultural Advertising *a choice of essays that he had written on his chosen profession and that they decided to print as his first contribution "The Farmer Wears Clothes." Yet Anderson somehow convinced the editors— who were, after all, business and social friends—to publish in the same issue of the journal a second essay by him under the pseudonym "Bert Sherwood"—an easily revealed disguise for the writer's seldom-used full name, Sherwood Burton Anderson. In contrast to the essay signed "Sherwood Anderson," the essay by "Bert Sherwood" assumed form as an imaginary letter from a traveling solicitor to his homebound wife, the wife herself being imaginary for the yet-unmarried young Anderson.*

2

Letters of an Advertising Solicitor to His Wife at Home

Agricultural Advertising 2 (February 1902): 36–37.

On Board C. B. & Q. "Eli," Feb. 15, '02

My Dear Wife:

Your note of the 10th was forwarded to me from St. Louis, and has helped me somewhat this week. However, you don't give me a fair shake on that Atwood deal, because I did try, and was not afraid of the game. Bluff old Jim Turner, with all of his years of experience and knowledge of the game, was just one too many for me. I simply had to beach the boat to keep from falling into the hands of the enemy. Of course, this does not mean that Jim Turner can do it again, for like the Yankee, when I saw he had me beaten, I turned in and watched to see how he did it. Next time I will have a different story to tell you, for I know fully forty tricks that our good friend Jim has never thought of. I have worked them all out since that afternoon in Atwood's office.

What did Jim say? Oh, he looked comfortable and happy and decidedly cocky, just as yours truly would have looked had he landed the business.

I sailed into Springfield this morning quiet and easy, with a watch-out from the conning tower for Jim Turner and his little round craft, but did not sight him. I suppose he will sail off down through the South Seas now and enjoy the fruits of his victory—$10,000. Ouch! It hurts yet, every time I think of it. I'll tell you, my dear, if we are going to make of ourselves a world power we have got to appropriate a lot of time and energy right now to getting some of the old leaks plugged up. Why, Jim had all sorts of new guns and smokeless powder, and all that kind of stuff, and he just simply raked me fore and aft.

I sat down last night and wrote a long letter to the house, telling them in detail just how it was all done, and then I tore it up and sent this telegram instead: "If you can hire Jim Turner at any price, you had better let me go." Of course, they were decent about it and wrote back that Jim Turner was a big, fat bluffer, but that does not lay any cooling hand on the hurt place. No one can really do that but you. Kind of funny how they fool a fellow sometimes, isn't it? Now, if anyone had written out that talk this big, fat, lazy-looking old boy put up, I should have sized up the author as a shrewd-looking, square-jawed, hungry-eyed Sherlock Holmes sort of a proposition. Why, it's getting so bad a fellow has to trim for action every time a tramp steamer sticks its dirty snout up in these waters. Guess I'll hire out as deck hand on some good, lively ferryboat.

I liked what you said about the advertisements. It shows, as your own old daddy would have said, that "you are fitten to be the wife of such a noble man." I don't care particularly for your criticism of the plow advertisement, though. It lacks knowledge of the chap we are after, the farmer. Those advertisements are for the March issues of the papers. Don't you remember how your old daddy used to settle himself down before the fire during those wet, cold March evenings and spend long hours poring over the advertising columns of the farm paper he has taken so long? Goodness knows, I remember them well enough, and bully well I wished the old codger would let the advertisements go hang, and be off to bed. I wonder sometimes if he would ever have given you up had he known what was in my mind at those times. Now, I am going to get even on some other poor youth by writing advertisements that will give the old fellow all the cold facts he wants. Apply the past to the future, my dear girl.

Bert Sherwood

If Sherwood Anderson wrote other columns for Agricultural Advertising *under pseudonyms less transparent than "Bert Sherwood," the disguises have not been revealed. Probably Anderson had delighted at seeing his own name in print as a sign of his professional and social success, and he had surely found out from writing advertisements and business letters and columns that words were powerful tools when used carefully and gracefully, for his next columns for* Agricultural Advertising *reveal a growing awareness of voice and audience that approaches a sense of stylistic sophistication.*

3

A Soliloquy

Agricultural Advertising 9 (April 1902): 25.

🍃 *Some take large* space in poor mediums; others take small space in good mediums, and still others take no space in any medium. And every man is wise in his day and generation, and the world wags merrily on.

Some advertising men shake their heads and look wise and depend on their proposition to carry them through; others toil terribly and carry a poor proposition to a profit-paying basis, and nearly all of them are human, after all, and quite a few eventually retire to the rear and slide quietly down upon the green plush.

I wonder after all if this advertising game isn't a good deal like the meat business, and the grocery business, and the clothing business, where the man who comes down early and stays down late is the man who finally gets the money—and the wrinkles. If after all it isn't a question of good, hard plugging early and late, and not much mystery or genius about it.

I know a man in the business now who is a genius; who has all the hall-marks; who has a sad, far-away look in his eye; who lets his hair grow long and allows his fingernails to remain untrimmed. Yet he doesn't seem to hit the high places.

Pshaw! I thought I was going to wake up some morning and find under my pillow a golden key that would unlock the door to advertising success, and here I have got to work, and eat ten-cent lunches, and make my small brother press my trousers, just as if I wasn't in the finest business on earth.

4

Writing It Down

Agricultural Advertising 9 (November 1902): 46.

❧ *Did you never*—best of workers—square up to your desk to do a task and find yourself, after half an hour's frantic effort, jabbing holes in the paper with your pencil and wishing with all your heart that you felt now as you did yesterday when you were talking to Smith or last night when you dined with Peterson?

Taking it for granted that it be true that our best thoughts come to us at odd moments how are we to make that momentary inspiration lasting? Write it down. On the margin of your newspaper, on the wrapping of your package of laundry, on the side of a convenient building even, but write it, write it again and again, if necessary. It can be temporarily forgotten then. It is yours, and it will come back.

Sometimes in reading we wade through half a book without our real selves being touched, when suddenly a sentence fairly leaps out of the page. That sentence belongs to us. It may be the only thing in the book that does belong to us, and if we lose it we have only ourselves to blame. Write it down.

Some time ago a college professor from the West wrote a song of labor that went ringing and ringing over the world. It aroused criticism because of its sentiment, but it wasn't easily forgotten. I read it once and I have awakened in the night, after a hard day's work, to find myself singing it over aloud. One day I saw a part of the original manuscript of this song. It was cut and patched terribly. Lines of it had been rewritten a dozen times. A word was cut out here and one inserted there. Do you suppose that man sat down and wrote that song while one class of gum-chewing girls filed out of the geometry class and another class filed in? Depend upon it he didn't. It came to him a line at a time at night by the fire; possibly a whole verse wrote itself during a night ride as he watched the moon and the lights of lonely farm houses fly by the car window. It took years. It took patience. But depend upon it, he wrote things down.[1]

And this naturally leads up to a suggestion concerning your advertising. Don't wait until the eleventh hour and then expect to sit down, or have some other man sit down, and do good work. Get your advertising man to you early. Talk things over with him, and then when anything good comes to either of you, you can not only write it down, but apply it on the spot.

1. Edwin Markham's poem "The Man With the Hoe," inspired by Jean-François Millet's 1863 painting "The Man With a Hoe," achieved national popularity after publication in 1899 in the *San Francisco Examiner*. The poem begins: "Bowed by the weight of centuries he leans / Upon his hoe and gazes on the ground. . . ."

5

Not Knocking

Agricultural Advertising 9 (December 1902): 22–23.

There's a lot of folks here who are dullards,
To whose eyes the light never climbs;
Let's accept them and own they are bone of our bone
And have sprung from the sins of our times. [1]

✺ *A few weeks* ago I rusticated for a day or two in a small village in one of our central western states. A beautiful little place it is, stored snugly away under a row of stately hills.

There are old mills there and water wheels and long half-decayed wooden bridges over a clear stream where there ought to be trout. A painter would grow opulent with material in this place, and yet it has never produced a painter. A corrupt politician, a conductor or two on the town's one railroad, and a long row of gray-haired old boys who sit in the sun down by the station are the only production of what the aforesaid politician calls "this gem of the hills."

I haven't mentioned John Brazleton, the man I went there to see, because he isn't a part of the town. He belongs to the hills and to the great world beyond the hills.

I slept in a little room up one flight of stairs in the "Empress Hotel." I sat tilted back in a chair in the barbershop and heard the postmaster tell obscene stories to the son of the grocery-man. I heard the old boys, who moved up en masse from the station to the hotel office at evening, discuss national affairs in a way that filled me with dread and apprehension. Roosevelt was a "grand-stand bluffer," Mitchell was in the employ of the coal barons, England—well, never mind what England was— and my friend John Brazleton was a "bluffer" and a fraud. [2] You cannot imagine how many times I heard that word "bluffer" used. This man or that man was a "bluffer" and had a "gift of gab." It was not only the whole explanation of Mr. Brazleton's success, but it was the soothing balm with which they bathed their own failures.

Now, there isn't anything remarkable about this town. You have lived in one like it no doubt, and you and I know that there are a lot of good, strong, simple people who live and die in such places. The point is that, in spite of the efforts of right-meaning editors, who send their literature into thousands of such towns, in spite of cheap books and good schools, the youths of these towns, in about nine cases out of ten, have an entirely wrong idea of what constitutes success. They think that this man or that man has succeeded because he is "slicker" than his brothers, because he is a "bluffer" and a clever cheat, because he is watching always to see whom he may hoodwink.

I mention this particular town because in it lives and works John Brazleton, a man known and respected through a dozen states for his ability, for his absolute integrity and for his bigheartedness and strength of character. There is something entirely dramatic and just a bit pathetic in the figure of this silent man surrounded by his books here among the hills, and the obscene postmaster and his ken. He is like a bit of the big world, where men work, thrown down here where men do rot, at the base of the beautiful hills, and yet this man went to school with the postmaster, he went fishing with the grocer, he whipped the corrupt politician on the public square, he smoked corn-silk cigarettes in the barn back of the school house, he grew up to manhood among them all, and then the world beyond the hills called him, and he went forth and came back a man.

In the western advertising field there are any number of John Brazletons. There are a few obscene postmasters who tell stories to grocers' sons, and there are decayed chaps who think the game is one of "bluff," who never see the hills of truth and who discredit every man who believes in his work and in the good of his work. You will hear such fellows talking much of "graft" and of having "worked" this man or that man for one, two or ten thousand dollars. You will hear them wisely declare that the John Brazletons are "smooth" or "slick" and have won the respect of men by their ability to cheat. It is such men who want to run your business, who are cock sure of things, who know the game from A to Z. You cannot tell them anything, because they are men "to whose eyes the light never climbs." It will be a good healthy day for the whole profession when such men all get back to their barber-shop and to a warm chair by the stove in the office of the "Empress."

1. Probably a verse from one of the newspaper poets of the day.
2. Theodore Roosevelt became president of the United States with the assassination of William McKinley 14 September 1901; in 1902 President Roosevelt began federal investigation of the activities of corporations for possible violation of antitrust laws. John Mitchell, president of the United

Mine Workers Union from 1889 to 1908, led a strike of anthracite coal workers in 1902. President Roosevelt had the federal government intervene in the strike to assure continuing coal supplies for American homes and businesses.

6

We Would Be Wise: Talking It Out

Agricultural Advertising 10 (January 1903): 45–47.

☞ *Originality in methods* and fertility of ideas are necessary to every man who would make a success in the game of advertising, and for this very reason new methods and new ideas are much sought, with, of course, the result that men sometimes grasp and spend their money lavishly on schemes that have neither convincing points nor the very necessary merit of directness. I have known men, however, with their hands on something good, with confidence in its success, and the ability to convince other men of its merits, kill the thing by the fear of talking it over with their fellows; men who could look at it with clear judgment and perhaps prevent the mistakes common to hot enthusiasm. Be sure of this: No man with ability to chisel a scheme into a bank account is going to steal what you have. In the first place he wants your help and is usually in a position to pay for what you have, and then he is apt to be an honest chap anyway and not given to stealing. We hear vague tales occasionally of some long-haired genius who has sold a million dollar idea for 75 cents, to the end that he might eat, but I have never met such a man and rather suspect that they are mostly in oblivion with the dodo bird. What care we if someone steal half the ideas that come to us, anyway? It were far better to let them go by the board and clear the decks for anything new that may come our way than to go hanging around an idea and nursing it in silence, and perhaps losing half a dozen good things because we have given too much time to one poor little scheme.

Then let's talk things out. Let's tell each other about our schemes and our hopes when we talk together. You may not get one practical suggestion from the solicitor who comes in and takes two hours of your time, but if you have talked heartily and wholesomely to him of your work, and have not wasted time with beating about the bush, you will find you have done yourself no end of good and strengthened your convictions and your courage by the very force of your own statements. Every man who takes this attitude and follows it persistently will, in the very nature of things, say and do a lot of things that will cause his brother to laugh the laugh of scorn, but what of that? How are we to grow in power and ability if we are not occasionally well roasted in the flames of ridicule? Let the mistake be a healthy one from a healthy mind and the laugh will be just as healthy, and will no doubt help us and prevent us taking ourselves too seriously.

Most anyone can stand a good, healthy, hearty fool who lets everyone know he is a fool, but your glum chap who is a fool "all to himself like," is the man who wrecks things and spoils other men's work.

& The size of the advertisement may represent the size of your pile. It doesn't necessarily represent the size of your future.

& You can't be too enthusiastic yourself. You can let the other fellow be too enthusiastic.

& The fear of being called a knocker keeps many an advertising man from trying to right known wrongs.

& When some men shake hands with you, you feel like asking them to hand it back.

& After all you're glad you're not a coal baron?

& I would rather be a mailing boy in the office of a winner than queen of the Philippine Islands. One couldn't be both.

& The man who can beat the old plan of telling the truth in a plain, direct way was around yesterday looking for a job.

❧ The result sheets of 1903 will make the prosperity stories of 1902 look like 30 cents.

❧ If you are going to be an advertising man drive your stake into something and say you originated it. They all do it.

❧ Good advertising is salesmanship boiled down.

❧ Better not succeed. When you have succeeded you're done.

❧ You'll be contented if you really know you're trying.

❧ In the army they have a way of calling the subordinate officer into the quiet of the commander's tent when they want to read the law and gospel to him. Don't call down the clerk or the salesman before the stenographers. It gives him a personal grievance that kills half the force of what you say. The quiet of the inner office makes strong words sink home.

❧ Hands were made to work with and not to hit heads with.

❧ I should like to have a noble past, but I should rather have a decent future.

❧ We don't want to show you. We want to help.

❧ Extend your follow-up system in 1903.

After the editors of Agricultural Advertising *had published six of Sherwood Anderson's columns in the first twelve months of his career as a writer, they agreed with the young businessman at the beginning of 1903 to publish a series of his columns under the general title "Rot and Reason." In the subsequent ten essays, as Anderson explored various aspects of the profession of soliciting and writing advertising copy, the young author's ambitions as a writer became more evident, for his situations became more and more dramatized, his characters became better developed, and his imagined emotions ranged beyond the scope of mere business essays.*

7

Rot and Reason

Agricultural Advertising 10 (February 1903): 13–14, 16.

THE NEW JOB

& *A new job*, a new place among new men.

"Men who know me not, not yet of my mistakes; ah, there I will do things. An end now to all carelessness and slighting of things. A new grip on the reins. New air in my nostrils, new men playing with me the game of business. I'll play fair now. Of course I have dodged a little from time to time, and there was that nasty winter when I stuffed reports to that little western house and had good work to get out without disgrace. But that was the girl's fault after all, and anyway, it's all over now and I have changed; at any rate I am going to change when I get well rid of this crowd here who never would give a fellow a decent show.

"I just had a talk with Walker, the manager over there, and he is all right, says there isn't anything I can't aspire to in their office. Mighty fine luck a chap has trying to get on here. They don't seem to think of anything except looking up his little mistakes; narrow that's what I call them and I am glad I am going. Of course you fellows are all right. The old man hasn't got it in for you and there isn't anyone jealous of you.

"Now, there's Dick Richards, well you know what I think of him; went and played me that scurvy trick about the general manager job. You see it was like this: I wanted to join a dancing club over on the North Side and I asked Dick to take part of my work during the rush; came down here and worked three nights a week for me; knew all along that the place was open to one of us and might have said something and not gone on posing as a martyr. Said he didn't know, but he did, that's what. There won't be any of that sort of thing over at Boose Bros., for I met all of the boys over there and they are mighty good fellows. We all went out and had a drink together and Boose drank right along with us just like one of the boys. You bet he'll give a fellow a chance."

Change! Change! Change! The pasture over the fence. The new strange land beyond the sun's going-down. Who among us hasn't longed for the place where we could begin anew, and who hasn't been shocked to find that it wasn't so fine after all? The chief in the new land has also his books and his book-keeper and there are footings-up and balancings-off at the end of the year. And the sheep are separated from the goats, the weeds from the good grain, and the asses from the thorough-breds, as in the old pastures.

The business house that doesn't hoe out the weeds won't raise the big crops and the man with the red heart of life in him don't want to be planted in the garden of the careless chief.

Johnson, of Johnson & Co., wants good men. Brown, of Brown & Co., is sad because he can't get winners. Thousands of good business men are abroad in every city, every village green, searching for hidden ability and because of this they gather in many promising youths and talk fine and fair to them, as though the garden of all desires was open to every man who went into Johnson & Co.'s plant.

And the youths rush in, and, finding the work as hard as the day is long, they listen to the bird song of Brown only to repeat the old story.

To the end of life Brown and Johnson will require that every man earn his salary (and rightly) and rightly or not, they will both have days when the uncertainties of business and the incompetence of employees will make them surly and dis-agreeable. And neither Brown nor Johnson will be surly to me if I am too valuable for Brown or Johnson to lose.

THE LAUGH OF SCORN

Any man, no matter what his station in life may be, who is in earnest about his work will always find plenty of people to make fun of his poor efforts. It is a way they have. The cynical, the weak, the incompetent and sometimes the brutally strong are prone to laugh long and loud at the earnest conscientious fellow. Sometimes the laugh is deserved and does good. Sometimes it isn't deserved and if our earnest fellow is inclined to take himself unusually serious, it hurts, and is wrong as is everything that cuts into the worker beside you.

But if our earnest fellow has a touch of humor in his makeup and a quiet twinkle in the corner of his eye, he will weigh that laugh, judge its effect on his ego and go merrily on his way toward the goal.

Brave, patient, earnest fellows, fighters for the firm and winners in the game, are constantly popping up out of the seething mass of us, and lo! us poor sightless ones who saw not the man nor the purpose of his work are glad indeed to proclaim him from the house tops.

THE TRAVELING MAN

The illustration is a faithful reproduction of the popular idea of the traveling salesman. It was stripped from a cover of an expense account book published in Detroit by a firm that should know better than to sling our past in our faces in this manner.[1]

I have no doubt this rare bird existed in some former time. My forebear tells me it did, and there are still signs of his muddy tracks in the minds of the populace. Stripped of the romance of his traveling, his loud clothes, his diamonds and his grip on the affections of dining room girls, he must have been a rare one indeed.

Common to the verge of imbecility, dressed as only a fool would dress nowadays, and having as his chief stock of trade a fund of vile and indecent stories, he went forth with his soap, his cigars and his ladies' underwear to smear the path of all decent men who must follow him for years to come. I have been told that occasionally specimens of this tribe may yet be found in all their unwashed unloveliness in out-of-the-way places about the country, but they are going, and thank Providence they will soon be gone.

And it isn't the house and it isn't his fellows who are causing this welcome death. It's tne new business man, the new manufacturer, the new buyer—clean, well read, clever men are not going to buy goods of fellows like our friend above when they can buy of their equals, of men who can be quiet, earnest and decent, even when away from home and with the eyes of high school girls upon them.

The world moves and to the man whose business sends him forth with bags and baggage, the best and most hopeful sign of its moving is the disappearance of "Noisy Johnny."

❧ It is usually safe to advise the man of small capital to stay out of advertising. If he is a winner he won't heed your advice, and if he is weak-kneed, your advice is good.

❧ The man who fails has all the fun ahead.

❧ Good work is fun. Why pat him on the back?

❧ You never spent an hour telling the truth earnestly and forcibly without gaining. If you did not convince the man you strengthened your own belief and perhaps the man was convinced without your knowing it.

❧ There is no worse bore in the world than the good man who thinks his own kind of goodness the best for everyone, unless it be the man who thinks the same about his particular kind of advertising.

❧ Make a man see and he'll do the work.

❧ No man ever finished his work. He does well if he finishes his hopings.

❧ The charm of advertising lies in the uncertainty that we were wont to curse.

❧ We are no better advertising men than we are good citizens.

❧ If you knew just how to do it you would have the office

boy doing the work while you slept. The uncertainty is what keeps you on your mettle.

✺ 'Twill soon be spring again.

1. The illustration accompanying Anderson's words is of a dashing salesman dressed in tall hat and colorful plaids and carrying a valise.

8

Rot and Reason

Agricultural Advertising 10 (March 1903): 18–20.

THE LIGHTWEIGHT

Vagrancy may not have increased, and the most reliable authorities are of the opinion that drunkenness is decreasing. Murders and suicides, however, have largely increased.—Recent newspaper comment.

✺ *The intense strain* of America's pellmell business life is breaking down the weak men and is, no doubt, the direct cause of many a fairly good man's downfall. Take the case of one of the men called in business parlance "a lightweight." He is, we will say, an ordinary, hard-working fellow with good enough intentions, with no great amount of will power and very little of the philosopher in his makeup; in short, a common man like the most of the rest of us, with a fair amount of ambition, a sprinkling of good, a shower of vanity, and the need of a job for his inheritance.

He is set down in a big office in one of our great commercial centers, given a desk near the door and fifteen minutes' talk on the possibilities of his one day becoming a Hill or a Gould and then left to work out his future among the stamps and letter files.[1]

Did you ever go to school with a fellow that could hit harder, jump higher and steal more melons than you? And didn't you most handsomely hate that fellow? Well, that is what our fellow by the door is going through now, except that instead of one there are dozens who can beat him at every turn.

If he were a bit of a philosopher, now, he would whistle something lively, stick grimly to his stamps and his files and after a time things would begin to brighten a bit. But he isn't a philosopher, you see, so he tells the stenographer of his grievance and he radiates to the other discontented spirits in the office, and then someday a jumper and a swimmer and a general all-around winner comes along, and our friend is out of a job.

He'll make news now if he isn't careful, for he's on a fair way to the horror column unless he meets a man who sees and knows. Our friend wants a bit of the helping hand, and he wants it now.

The gleam of light, the saving fact is that there be men, quick, hard, strenuous fellows, who don't take much stock in "the survival of the fittest" proposition and who are in business to better it rather than to pound a fortune out of it.

Business wants more such spirits, wants more newspaper editors, more editors, more workers who can shut their eyes to the main chance occasionally and work for the game itself. Let's stick to the strenuosity, let's stick to the pound and the grind and the general hurrah for things, but let's take a look at the heads we hit and stop occasionally to engender a little ginger and hope into the limber-legged fellow beside us, "the lightweight."

We'll balance up all right in the end. We'll do our share toward making this the biggest and brightest spot on the whole black earth, and we'll now and then make a winner out of a possible suicide. It's all a question of knowing and teaching, for the average business man isn't given to hitting his fellows in the face. But you know and I know that some of the cruelest moves in the day's work are made by cheerful enough fellows who go whistling through the market place, totally unconscious of the wrong they have done.

THE BORN QUITTER

"Poor old Johnson, he's all in," said the sandy-haired one, pointing at Johnson hurrying up the street with his coat held tightly about his throat for lack of buttons.

A bit of rough going up the back stretch, a smash over the nose from a riding whip and the not over-strong heart broke.

"Johnson is all in."

And it wasn't the boss and it wasn't the men below; it was his equals, God help them, and it is the equal, the man who ought to be a brother, who breaks thousands of hearts in the rough running up the back stretch of every day's business race. It's easy enough when you swing around the corner and face the wire. They're all watching you then and shouting and throwing things in the air, and the keen-eyed fellows in the stand have their eye on everything and everyone. But back there in the dark, Mr. Clerk, away back in the ruck there, you want a big heart and divine faith, if you are ever to be a derby candidate.

"Ah! let 'em cut and heal," says the sandy-haired one. "How are we ever to find the worthy man if all these weak hearts are not sent back about their business and done with it? Ride hard," say I. "Crowd hard; play the game. I don't want always to mill around in all this rucky push. I want to get clear or be smashed and the story over."

Yes, Mr. Sandy, but who was your sire? What green fields did you roam in your colthood? What wise old mother talked to you down by the big trees at evening? Johnson, you know, was born of a surly sorrel in the winter time and the wolves snapped up his mother's soul one night in his yearling days.

Let's reconsider Johnson and this smashing business. Not but what we ought to ride hard and whoop things up—that's what's making winners of us—but when we're away back there in the dark and the crowd is listening to the band and the judges can't see, and there isn't a soul looking, let's just smash Johnson over the rump instead of the nose.

❧ If you could be the best advertising man in the United States twenty years from now, would you be happy? Or do you want to be President? Both jobs ought to pay about the same.

❧ A good enemy will help you as much as a good friend.

❧ "I wish I had a friend honest enough to tell me when my stuff was rotten." I said this to a Philistine and he told me it was all "rotten."

❧ In the next cell below the "knocker," you will find the man who is always complaining because someone has "knocked" him.

❧ Do not buy duplicate circulation. If a man reads your advertisement twice he might believe it.

❧ Said the lily to the rose: "Why do all the bees visit you and gossip at your door?" "Because," replied the rose, as it scattered its perfume into the desert air, "I advertise."

❧ A man's saying that he believes in the world does not necessarily mean that he is a credulous fool.

❧ Good advertising counts; good form letters help; good literature is necessary, but a good advertising man there must be to win with all these.

❧ As between valuable scientific information and watery sentiment, the Farm Paper Editor must hesitate long. He is at times almost forced to believe that people do like slush.

❧ The successful man is not wrecked in the wreck. The unsuccessful man is wrecked by success.

❧ The Spaniard who originated the phrase "Yankee pig" must have traveled in the spit-besmeared smoking car of one of our passenger trains.

❧ Do not get into the habit of putting papers on your list because "they don't cost much." This is a mighty poor argument for a paper to use.

1. James J. Hill, United States financier, head of the Great Northern Railway from 1893 to 1912; George Jay Gould, son of the pioneering financier Jay Gould, became head of the Missouri Pacific Railroad and the Texas and Pacific Railroad in 1893.

9

Rot and Reason

Agricultural Advertising 10 (April 1903): 12, 14.

DOING STUNTS

❧ *Back in the* small towns of Ohio and Kentucky twenty years ago they had a class of horses called "quarter horses." They used to get them out on Saturday afternoons and literally tear up the ground between Perkins' corner and the grocery store. Everybody turned out and whooped things up, and sometimes the tavern-keeper would bet as much as three dollars against Bill Enright's sorrel (first having a quiet talk with Bill).

It is said that these horses could beat anything living for the distance, but no one owned a stopwatch then, and the horses never lasted long or did a decent whole mile, so this is doubtful.

My, but it was exciting though! Slamming down through between the farm buildings and the row of farm wagons; and a race won made the winner the village hero and got him talked about for at least a month at every livery stable.

I often wonder how many of us are "quarter horses" and are doing stunts among the store boxes. And whether, if turned square about, we could do one good long heart-breaking mile. 'Tis satisfying, I will admit. Have done a few myself and then bought fellows' lunches so I could tell about it. But it won't put our man high up among advertising men like facing the game and working hard day and night through the years. It's cheap, too. For never was there a quarter horse, a doer of stunts, who couldn't be bought by an inn-keeper for one dollar and fifty cents.

PACKINGHAM

In the village of Omaha, on the trail of the tourist, there lived and worked one Packingham, a short, broad-shouldered man with a merry eye and a foolish fondness for his work and his firm.

Now, it's all right to be loyal, but Packingham was more than loyal. He was a fool. He did all the work that anyone wanted him to do and then went back and did some more just for fun. The stenographers grew wroth with him and the night-watch, who wanted to lock up and go down and tell the engineer how the Gray Eagle ran in the third, positively hated him. He used to refuse to dance after midnight because he wanted to have a steady eye in his head when he talked to Prowler, of the Union Pacific, in the morning. He was good to Mrs. Packingham, but, as people often said, she was almost as big a fool as he.

Packingham had a beautiful theory about his work and his attitude toward his firm and it went something like this:

"Because my work is more to me than anything else in the world, I will make it my religion. When I am tempted to be full of sin and unclean, I will remember that such a course would make my work full of sin and unclean. When I am tempted to lie and cheat, I shall expect the bookkeeper to lie and cheat. When I'm lonely and sad on moonlight nights, I'll just come down here and this old job and I will have a good long social evening together, then perhaps when I die I will go to some place where a fellow will not have to waste so much time sleeping."

In the fullness of time Packingham became known in the land, and men said that although the poor chump knew nothing but work, he certainly did know that. He developed a scheme for turning a lot of pig iron into a machine used in the families of the humble, and this machine, which worked just like Packingham, enabled his firm to capture the market and sell something for two dollars that had formerly cost six or eight. He did about everything but talk about himself and then the thing happened that gained him his title of "fool."

A trust lawyer took the morning train over into New Jersey one morning and came back some time later with the charter for The American Amalgamated Labor Saving Wringer Co. in his pocket and a beautiful and devilish plan for disposing of the stock in his head.

Because the name of Packingham was big in the wringer line he took another train for Omaha that night. At Omaha he was joined by one Wescott, a very dear friend and earnest adviser of Packingham, and together they descended on the silent man of work.

Now, all the talk and all the advice of New Jersey and Wescott would take much space, so we will simply say that they offered Packingham thirty-five thousand a year and a two hundred thousand dollar bonus if he would desert his firm and come into the Amalgamated. Not only offered it, but arranged to put the entire amount into the hands of whomever Packingham might name. And Packingham's salary was just five thousand a year. And Packingham laughed and went home and told Mrs. Packingham and she laughed. Wasn't he a fool?

❧ There was an old fellow at home that hoed corn. He was grim, grey and silent, but because he pleased my boyish heart I was glad to hoe beside him for the dignity of his presence. One hot day when we had hoed to the end of a particularly long and weedy row and were resting in the shade by the fence he put his big hand on my shoulder and said, "Don't the corn make you ashamed, Sherwood, it's so straight?"

❧ Of No Value
  • A system in the hands of an unsystematic man.
  • A friend who demands no manhood in you.
  • A wife who inspires you to no better work.
  • Money you have not fairly earned.

- Fame got by trickery or a pose.
- Advertising that you are going to do when you have got more money than you know what to do with.

❧ Chicago Inspirations

- The morning sun shining on the Field Columbian museum.
- The lake front at night with the lights of the trains and the lake ahead, and the roar of the city behind.
- The front platform of an elevated train going around the Union Loop.
- The view on Upper State Street at night.
- The new office of *Agricultural Advertising,* in the Powers Building.

10

Rot and Reason

Agricultural Advertising 10 (May 1903): 20, 22.

UNFINISHED

❧ *The life of* every busy man who really gets into the game is one everlasting, unceasing effort to catch up the broken strings of things, tie the ends and feel at last that there is something finished, something done. In this as in everything else worthwhile, no man really succeeds. A few clever, clocklike men appear to succeed, but they don't. And the great mass of us never even make a showing of success. Enthusiasm follows enthusiasm in hot succession; dream follows dream; and the life's ambition of today is left broken and torn on the Jericho road while we with eager eyes are tearing and scraping at the obstacles on some ever-endless path.

Morning finds the advertising man full of the spirit of "get things done," but alas, what a sorry mess it is when the rattling machines cease their rattling and the office boy has gone for the night, Smith's letter unanswered, Colver's copy unfinished, issues missed. An endless, heart-breaking mess it is, lapping always into the next day, the next month and the next year.

In the first waking sickness of it, how many the good men who have felt like dropping the whole thing and going out to find a healthy, reasonable job as end man on a sewer contract. A most hopeful, cheerful beggar he is, the advertising man, seeing his hardest licks go smash, his cleverest lines muddled and his finest talk interrupted. And how decent he is about it in the end. Day after day, week after week, year after year, he faces his own failures and yet believes down in the heart of him that he is in the greatest business on earth and that next year will set all straight and turn all his penny marbles into diamonds.

It seems to advertising men that their work is particularly unfinishable and it is true that ever and ever the new is taking the place of the old, but who among them would change it? Gray old veterans will shake their old heads and with withered finger under your nose talk of the days to come when advertising shall come into its own just as though they too had all the work ahead.

It makes a man glad he is alive and young now and it makes him doubly glad that he is in even such an unfinishable business as advertising.

FINDING OUR WORK

We all hear more or less talk about the good fortune of the man who has found his work. It is a thing much discussed by school teachers and mothers with sons out of a job, but not much heard of in the man talk of the office and the shop.

Of course not every man can sell goods. Not every man can run a lathe. And very few men can successfully run a business. But I think it true in the great majority of cases, it isn't so much a question of finding your work as it is of finding yourself, your faith, your courage.

Your really successful man is he who runs the lathe well, who in some way manages to make sales, who does well with a set of books, and who in good time makes himself felt as the director of all these. He does these things well because he believes the work at hand is his work and believing gives it his love and throws about it all of that glamour that comes to any place where a strong man works.

The average man looking for work to love is much like a certain acquaintance of mine (only that this was an honest chap) who used to stretch himself and lazily say that he would like to be in a place where a man could roll down to work about 11:30, look over his correspondence and then about 1:30 roll back home.

We are all chasing shadows no doubt, shadows of love, shadows of art, shadows of death, but there is no need chasing the shadow of my work.

God intended us to be a cracking good office boy, a wide-awake, careful clerk, an earnest, conscientious salesman, and finally, perhaps, an understanding, fearless boss. But he didn't intend us to go pining through the day and moaning through the night because we could find no work to love.

Let's save our pining and our moaning for our love affairs and be brave and cheerful about the work. It takes so much time out of our lives, and then perhaps if we are brave and clean and true, our work will appear there in the midst of the work at hand.

❧ It only takes years to solve the unsolvable.

❧ The busiest man has time to be the best friend.

❧ Every good advertisement is a nail in the structure.

❧ The man who means what he says is a good man. It does not matter whether he says it as well as the other fellow, or not.

❧ If you don't think more of yourself than you make known

you had better begin.

🙰 Every Monday morning begins a new advertising year.

🙰 There was a moment when the battle of Waterloo wavered in the balance. There were doubtful hours in the hot grain fields of Gettysburg. There are always shaky days in the successful advertising campaign when the quitter quits and the winner prepares for another charge.

11

Rot and Reason

Agricultural Advertising 10 (June 1903): 54, 56–57.

Knock and the world knocks with you.
Boost and you boost alone.—B.L.T. [1]

KNOCK NO. 1

🙰 *From the first* conception of the advertising magazine, writers have written articles to prove that the man who lets his advertising lag during the hot months is making a serious mistake, and to keep everlastingly at it has become a sort of patent phrase that falls trippingly from the tongues of both the wise and conservative, the foolish and unthinking. If the writer means by this to counsel the advertiser to keep "at it" unceasingly year after year, the advice is good and wise enough, although having been so bantered about, it probably won't add one cubit to the stature of the man who utters it. If, on the other hand, he is merely trying to pat the man on the back to the end that his columns may be filled during the silly season, he is a hold-up man with sample copies of his burglar-kit in his hip pocket.

The writer's attention was recently called to a case. An advertiser with an article that the farmer uses early in the spring when he is preparing for his spring plowing was strongly advised to ignore his own judgment and, cutting down his list of papers, run his advertising for a longer period in a smaller list. As a result this advertiser lost something like a thousand dollars, when before he had been able to close the season some five or ten thousand to the good.

Advertising, like every other well established proposition, is gradually accumulating a lot of stock expressions or proverbs that are picked up and used by the thoughtless, regardless of their true meaning. Of course, the better men know well enough that each particular proposition is a problem in itself and must be analyzed and studied before a decision can be given. Even then the best of men in closing his year's work can look back to many a spot where they have done the things they ought not to have done, and left undone the things they ought to have done.

KNOCK NO. 2

If you love the West, a trip in the East will make you jealous for your West. If you love the East, the West will make you ashamed of yourself. And to have been born a New Yorker and never to have seen the sun shining on the prairies or never to have known a rough, hearty, western friend is as unfortunate as to have been born a westerner and never to have realized how much they have that we need.

To the western man the East smacks of self-satisfaction, of something very like complacency. It smiles wisely and pities you because you are from the West, and the smile hurts because there are good reasons for that same smile.

Speaking advertisingly, it would seem to one who forms his opinions from but fleeting glances that the East has far to go before it will produce anywhere near as much agricultural advertising as does the West, but it will do it and more, eventually. Back in inner offices all over the East, it is safe to venture, there are men looking on at the game, and someday they will come into our field and do things in a big way. And they'll do it well too, for they'll come out here and hire western men to do it for them.

In a country where there is a town (western "city") every ten miles, and where the factory smoke of one of these towns soils the linen of the business men of the next, and where everywhere, all about, there are factories which should be using farm paper space—there in such a land, there are advertising possibilities that look like mountains to the western fellow who is used to having a week's soliciting scattered over a half dozen states.

BOOST NO. 1

As a man travels about he realizes, more and more, that the business man is the very front and center of things American. He is the man on horseback in our national life. He knows and, I pray you, doubt not that he dictates the whole works. William Allen White has recently shown in a brilliant series of articles in the *Saturday Evening Post* that a little group of brainy business men rule the Senate and House of Representatives.[2] The business man rules the stage; our literature is molded to his needs and "good business" brings to us and keeps on our shores the great European musicians. And what manner of man is he, this American business man? Is he a better, cleaner and braver man than the warriors and scholars who have cast their big shadows in the past? You can be sure he is. He may have occasionally a bad dose of dollarism, but he takes care of his family; he educates his sons, he loves one woman, and he usually knows that honesty is as a solid wall, and truth as a shining light.

Greatness didn't die with Cæsar, nor with Abe Lincoln, and always among the dominating class of a great people there are great men, and just as sure as is the fact of the business man's power, just so surely will this age produce its truly great individuals, and the place to look for them is among business men.

They probably won't play much to the grandstand, nor make epigrams before they die, but whether they be in cotton, in corn, or in advertising, they'll be there, and the Negro question, the labor question and other things that do ripple the surface of things will be settled quietly and firmly in good time by that great force—the American business man.

ᴈ A man can spend his time counting stars or he can camp out with the street sparrows and I think he'd better do the first, only he had better keep his eyes open while the stars sleep.

ᴈ Every forward step in knowledge of ourselves must lead toward charity for others.

ᴈ In every square advertising deal there are four sides—the advertiser's side, the publisher's side, the agency's side and the general public's side. The game, of course, is to try and see all these four sides with equal clearness.

ᴈ If God doesn't make many Abraham Lincolns he doesn't make many Booths either, for that matter.[3]

ᴈ The seeming incompetence of all men in some things only makes them human after all.

ᴈ Advertising space is as inexhaustible as the sky. Sometimes it comes about as high.

ᴈ "Does the stock man wear boots in summer?" asked Jerry, the artist. "Of course not," answered Major Critchfield. "Well, why don't he?" grumbled Jerry. "It would make him look so much better in a drawing."

1. "B.L.T." is probably Bert Leston Taylor, author of popular epigrammatic comic verse.

2. William Allen White, famous newspaper editor in Emporia, Kansas, in the period Anderson is discussing, published two political essays in the *Saturday Evening Post*—"The Politicians" in the issue of 14 March 1903 and "The President" in the issue of 4 April 1903.

3. John Wilkes Booth assassinated President Abraham Lincoln 14 April 1865.

12

Rot and Reason

Agricultural Advertising 10 (July 1903): 22–23, 26.

OFFICE TONE

❧ *As is the* number and variety of offices and the gilded and plain entrances thereto, so is the number of sensations in the mind of the solicitor as he enters. The imposing and flowery place where gold mines are sold; the dust-laden place where accounts are kept in the proprietor's hip pocket; and the modest, neat little place where the wife keeps books. And there are big, earnest, strenuous places where things are done and where you have to have your story well in hand, tell it and get **out**.

After some hundreds of these offices, of more or less note, the solicitor becomes possessed of a sort of sixth sense that tells him when he enters a place whether it will be well for him to rush in and shake the boss enthusiastically by the hand, or send in his card in a dignified way, the while he cools off his heated heels.

This something in the air, this general impression a place gives, might well be called "office tone," rather a high-sounding expression for everyday use, but it is the best the writer knows. This tone isn't purchased with the furniture nor rented with the place; it is a something as indefinite and vague as the thing about a man called "character," and yet it leaves a lasting impression and often determines the whole course of action to be followed in recommending a line of credit.

I know a place where the strength and fineness of this "office tone" braces a man like a dose of tonic or a fishing trip, and it has got into the blood of every man, from the president to the office boy, till they all love the place and find it no hardship to work there. And the "office tone," like every other strengthening thing about a business, gets into that firm's output and into their literature and into their advertisements, and stamps them, just as the place stamps itself on the mind of the visitor.

Did you ever go into the great retail establishment of Marshall Field & Co., in Chicago? Has tone, hasn't it? What did it? What makes the place so perfectly balanced? Undoubtedly the fact that at the head of it is a great merchant.[1] What makes the manufacturing place so like a beautiful, harmonious clang of industry and brains? A great manufacturer. What makes anything swing along with tone and harmony in this world? Great and harmonious men. There's where "office tone" comes from, for a jangled, crosswire kind of a man never gave tone to anything. Get into tune and your office will have tone and you will sing your advertising song in the right key.

FUN AND WORK

Men without experience in long living have always been the most prone to write of life and its fruits. And if you want a fine and complete system of morals that will solve all the difficult problems that do shadow the face of things, go to your healthy young thinker of twenty-five or thereabouts. For the same reason it is the young man, the stripling, the fellow just out of college, who can tell you the most about the ethics of business. Beardless young fellows of less than thirty settle more things in an hour at lunch than can the gray-haired old president in a fortnight. Of course they don't stay settled, and the truths of five and twenty bring grim smiles to their author at fifty. Here, however, is a bit given the writer by a young advertising manager that seems worth repeating. He was discussing the question of a man's duty to his business, and how much of his time and his thoughts belonged to his firm. "I'll tell you," he said, "a fellow's attitude should be like this. He should consider his business career as a sort of never-ending adventure, a thing of changes and chances, a thing likely at any time to lead to fortune or failure. And he should be game enough to accept either cheerfully. When you say to me that [if] I have only to sit on this bench and add up enough columns of figures so that I do it with extraordinary skill and precision I have succeeded, you are far from the mark—for me. I am a fellow with a love of hills and ravines and stretches of treacherous ground, and a dead-level road always did set me gaping. Of course, I'm just as likely to swing into a hole and be done as to cut along the edge to high safe ground, but at least I shall have added zest to my life and given my heart an eagerness for the day's work. Give me the man who thanks his God when a day begins rather than when it closes, who goes eager to his office, who gets as much fun and knowledge out of today's failure as from tomorrow's success. I want to love my work because it supplies me with bread and butter, I want to laugh and sing and fight and win and lose, and I want to get a lot of good fun out of the whole business. The point is that doing the work well that you love isn't work, it's fun, the best sort of fun, the very meat and kernel of life.

WORK IN THE DARK

About once a week the advertising agency gets a letter that reads something like this:

"I am selling hand organs. What percent can I allow for advertising?" What, indeed! The moon is blank miles from the earth. What does it cost to make a pound of green cheese?

And yet, this man is just the fellow who will get a line on plans of an advertising agency, let them make designs, get up copy, write follow-up letters, make up a list, and then go out and place his business with someone who can handle business at 2 percent, because the only service he gives to the advertiser is the service of a stenographer who sends out the orders.

"I am in trouble with Neighbor Jones. Enclosed find $5 for which please tell me how to beat him." What would you think of the man who sent that into a law office? And yet the two cases are not so different.

The advertising agency that tries to do its work well gives to every client's proposition as much care and study as the average law firm gives to the consideration of the cases that come under its supervision.

What does your article sell for? What percent of this is profit? What are you doing and what have you done to interest your dealers? What territory do you cover and what territory can you cover, without being eaten up by freight rates? How do you follow up inquiries and how can you afford to go down the road after the man who is trying to get away without buying? What particular class of folk and what particular section of the country have been your best buyers? What were your best selling months last year?

These are some of the things the agency wants to know; or better yet, they want to come to you and sit down at your desk and get at the heart of things, for the agency's man does not like to send you a half-hearted answer to your letter, any more than he wants to take your advertising if he does not think his firm can do you good and make your advertising pay you. They are mighty near as square a lot of men as you will find, the agency fellows, and they try to do their work well, but they do want you to take them into your confidence and give them a decent chance.

We would resent the suggestion that our firm was not an influence, then why not resent the thought that we—you and I—are not also an influence? We are part of the machine, part of the office force, workers in the big mill called America. I, for one, would be loath to cover myself with the odium of shirking it or laughing it away.

What are American advertising men? Well, to tell the truth, they are rather decent, earnest, clever fellows, who make a good living for themselves, and for those they love, and they know how to work, better than most.

When America is the biggest and finest country on earth, the world is going to look to the manners and hearts of American business men, and the groan or cheer depends upon what they see there.

One good way for a man who has made millions by under-paying those about him to square himself and relieve his name of all possibility of odium is by presenting certain pieces of money to his employees.

The difficult thing for a man with a victory won to under-stand is that it is not the money, but the touch, the power, the faith that the man in the middle distance is seeking.

1. Known for his business integrity and pioneering retailing practices in selling dry goods, Marshall Field established Marshall Field & Co. in Chicago in 1881.

13

Rot and Reason

Agricultural Advertising 10 (August 1903): 22, 24–25.

THE GOLDEN HARVEST FARMER

❧ *In England in* the days of good Queen Bess there developed a lot of old chaps who used to sit around coffee houses and say things for the benefit of posterity. These men are counted the finest developed of their age, and certain of us are wont to sigh that we did not live then, so that we could have gone to Cheshire Cheese, or some other place, and enacted the part of the barefoot boy worshipping at that shrine of wisdom. From all accounts we have of these fellows some of them must have been rather "swatty" looking, with egg on their waist-coats. Hardly any of them worked and none of them paid their taxes.

In America, in this age of the good, strenuous Theodore, we have a special development of our own.[1] He does not hang around grocery stores, or taverns, and he does not write stuff to give school boys a headache a hundred years from now, but he is a mighty fine chap and a model that the age and America can well be proud of. You will see him, as conceived by Jerry of the Art Department, on the front page, and as he stands there with folded arms, amid his grain piles, he is rather a fine article. This man, the farmer of the Twentieth Century, is the result of owning his own farm, of being his own boss, of electing his own Congressmen, and of generally running things for himself.

In the good old days that we were just talking about, a farmer was the last thing a man wanted to be. They used to buy and sell and trade them off with the place. They went with the land. They were in about the same standing as a good, well-built cowshed. Now, wouldn't you have a merry time trying to trade off Jim Bodsford, of Green County, Iowa, with the farm? Notice the way he turns up his chin; a balance in the bank did that. Look how he squares his shoulders back; a son in the State University did that. He is a dandy, a winner, a freeholder, a man, a farmer, and we who make a living trying to sell him goods have got to get up and dust, if we are going to keep pace with him.

Is it to be wondered at that the President of the Frank B. White Company is thinking day and night of how to improve the quality of the work sent out? Is it to be wondered at that he keeps about him the kind of men who can write stuff that will appeal to the honorable, husky and square Jim of Green County? And isn't it a worthy idea right now, at the golden harvest of the year, for the manufacturer and manufacturer's employees to take a brace and realize anew that Mr. Straightback Jim is about 95 in the shade and the sun is shining these days?

If I were Jerry, though, and had had the job of drawing that Golden Harvest Farmer, I should have made a stream of golden dollars running through his fingers, for that is what is going on all over the country. They have much monies on the farms in these days of 1903, but they are taking care of it, and the man who sells to them and starts the golden stream flow-ing his way has got to talk turkey straight from the shoulder in his advertisements, his letters and his literature.

GOLDEN HARVEST MANUFACTURERS

And how is the American manufacturer prepared to take care of the demands arising among the prosperous American farmers? Well, as old Thad used to say, "Some air and some ain't."[2] In the first place, the manufacturer, if he gives to his business the amount of attention and time necessary to make it successful, is very apt to think of the farmer as the same fellow he knew when he was a barefoot boy some thirty or forty years ago. He loses track of the fact that while he has been improving his methods and his mind, the farmer has been doing the same thing. His, the farmer's, golden harvest doesn't consist alone of more dollars in the bank, but also of new opportunities in the way of self improvement, both mental and physical. Independent living and independent financial conditions breed independent and searching thought, and the man who would reach an ideal must not be satisfied to have a subordinate edit the introduction and body of his catalogue with scissors and paste pot.

You know, in the days of scissors and paste pot farm papers, the scissors and paste pot catalogue may have been all right, but publishers of farm papers have realized long since that the day for this sort of thing has passed.

Not long ago a manufacturer, who wanted to send out form letters to a list of names of farmers, asked the writer to furnish him some copies of letters used by other manufacturers. Of course he was told that this could not well be done, but that the company would be glad to write some original letters for him. "Oh, no" [he] replied, "that's too much trouble. I can use the same ideas that the other fellow uses."

The writer doesn't contend that many manufacturers have not in every way kept abreast of the times, but he does believe that in the department of their business that ought to tell their story, many are woefully behind that farmer, and it doesn't pay, for golden harvest farmers ought to make golden harvest manufacturers.

THE GOLDEN FAKE

Suppose you had a client down in Indiana who sold wheelbarrows. Suppose when you first called on him he was spending about two hundred a year and was afraid of his own shadow. You call on him two or three times, and he begins to understand that you don't want to steal the inkstand, and makes an appropriation. You go about it carefully and make him up a nice list of good strong papers, fix him up some winning letters, go through his catalogue and generally spend about twice as much in hotel bills as you can expect to get out of him this year, and he is satisfied and happy and ready for a good year's business.

Now about this time along comes Eddy Scalper of the National Fake Advertising Company and solicits Mr. Wheelbarrow Manufacturer's advertising. Having ascertained finally and definitely that the business is placed and the contract signed and there is no possibility of his getting the business, Mr. Eddy takes on a saintly cast of countenance and asks: "And Mr. Wheelbarrow Manufacturer, how much is that list of papers going to cost with that firm?" "Five hundred and fifty dollars," says Mr. Wheelbarrow. "Isn't that strange? Now, I could have placed that same list for four hundred and eighty." Nice sort of work, isn't it? Of course it doesn't hurt Eddy that he has quoted it for less than cost. He can take a train and get out of town, and anyway he wouldn't take the business at his own figures. He has, however, managed to discredit an honest man trying to do his work decently and he is nice and proud and gleeful. This is merely quoted as the kind of Golden Harvest man not to be. May the day soon come when the breed is dead.

• Opportunity is a giddy bird and many colored. The trouble is that many of us are blind.

• Emerson said that if you did some one thing better than your neighbor the world would make a path to your door, even though you lived in a forest; but Emerson wasn't in the mail order business.[3]

• Advertisements are the dealer's show windows for the farmer and other out-of-town customers.

• I read a life of Lincoln and all the time I kept thinking what a good advertising man he would have been; then I read a life of Gladstone and I thought the same thing and Davy Crockett's left the same impression in my mind.[4] I guess any one of them would have been able to hold down a job.

• The fact that financial advertising isn't always crooked is often put forth as an argument in its favor.

• The man who makes a good article and advertises it honestly is helping the progress of the world.

• If you do something wrong, keep still about it. If you do good work, let the world know.

• Mennen doesn't have his picture on the box because he thinks he's handsome.[5]

• Many a man is blamed for keeping silent. Suppose he has nothing to say.

• Harvesting is the time for rejoicing. Let's.

1. President Theodore Roosevelt encouraged enjoyment of outdoor activities and had celebrated such life in *The Strenuous Life and Other Essays* (1900).

2. Anderson is recalling Thad Hurd, grocer in Anderson's boyhood town of Clyde, Ohio, and father of Herman Hurd, Anderson's closest boyhood friend.

3. Ralph Waldo Emerson wrote, in his *Journal* for February 1855: "If a man has good corn, or wood, or boards, or pigs, to sell, or can make better chairs or knives, crucibles or church organs, than anybody else, you will find a broad hard-beaten road to his house, though it be in the woods."

4. William Gladstone was four times Prime Minister of Great Britain; the American frontier hero Davy Crockett published his *Autobiography* in 1834.

5. William Mennen, head of the Mennen Company of Morristown, N. J., maker of cosmetic and personal-care products.

Although Sherwood Anderson may have been ethically displeased and professionally hurt by some of the disreputable practices in his chosen profession of advertising, he was kept on in his company when, in September 1903, the Frank B. White Company became the Long-Critchfield Company. And, fortunately for the literary ambitions of the young author, the new organization encouraged their bright and eager young writer to continue his columns in Agricultural Advertising.

14

Rot and Reason

Agricultural Advertising 10 (October 1903): 17–19.

TWENTY YEARS IN THE WEST

‹∎ *It happened to* be my good pleasure some time ago to read a book, *Across the Plains,* by Robert Louis Stevenson, in which our Iowa, Nebraska and Kansas was pictured as a bare, flat country, where man lived as on a billiard board with nothing of agreeable variety in all of the land about him, only flat dead stretches of barren acres, endless and extending from sun to sun.[1]

A most ghastly picture this, but what a triumph for the hardy Swede, German and Yank in the picture these same plains present today. There is color enough there now. There is enough of display, enough of the trappings of life, and the hum of machinery breaks the silence of a land green, blue and golden with its freight of crops. Prosperous towns stand asphalted and electric-lighted where thirty years ago a lonely eating house marked the beginning of another day's travel. Farm houses are already being occupied by the second generation and have acquired the settled look of homes in the East. Why carp of hard times in such a land? Why look for failure when the ground itself seems disposed to do its part? Of course, the city man, reader of stock gambling-influence crop reports, can figure you out a dismal winter, but I have yet to hear the echoes of this dismal talk in the country itself. You can by constant calamity howling make a depression in the city, but you will not succeed in the country for the simple reason that the country is not ready for the prophet of evil.

Such statements as these are at best impressionistic. From a railroad, a man does not get the truest expression of a country, but there is something in the air, an unrest, a muttering, that goes with hard times, that is entirely missing in the West today.

While traveling along one stretch of country there sat in the seat with me a fat, rosy little man, who, having found a good listener, told me, at great length and flourish, the history of the farms we passed, how thirty years ago they were just a flat, dead, billiard board land of western stories. Then how people came and took their one hundred and sixty [acres] of Government land and something of the hardships they suffered. For the rest he left me to look at the beautiful rolling fields of grain and corn as to how well they had finally prospered.

From your point and our point, this is the best possible kind of a country. When a land is brand new, man lives simply, with few tools for his trade and few luxuries for his living, but as neighbors thicken about him, his land becomes fenced and he begins to walk the accustomed paths of his own field and his energies are bent toward the higher development of his particular plot of ground. The use of fertilizers with their accompanying tools and machinery comes into his scheme of things. He requires more complicated tools for the stirring up of his soil, better to pulverize it and fight out the weeds. The struggle of the middle states farmer becomes his struggle and he becomes open for the argument of the middle states manufacturers of agricultural implements.

WHAT HENRY GEORGE SAID TWENTY YEARS AGO

It is interesting to note that, twenty years ago, no less a man than the great Henry George made a speech, in which he declared that the day when employees might hope to become employers had passed, interesting because the last twenty years has seen more men spring from poverty to affluence than any other like period in the history of the world.[2]

There is the labor question and the Negro question and the ever present money question, to be sure, and meanwhile the business men of the world go quietly ahead by this and that expedient, doing the work of the week and the day, while the reformers and the preachers and the politicians talk and mix new cure-alls for the ailing body politic. One good, clean-minded business man, who gets down to his work cheerfully in the morning, who treats the people about him with kindness and consideration, who worries not about world-politics, but faces the small ills of his day and the people about him, who tries to understand the janitor with his cap in his hand as well as the corporation manager and who sees the manhood in both, is probably doing more downright good than all of the canting moralists that ever breathed. Just as truly as the petty greed and selfishness of individuals and not anarchy and revolution work the destruction of nations, just that surely will cheerfulness and industry in the individual do their part of the work for the nation's prosperity. Every man is a unit in the nation and a unit in the firm. The firm is smaller, and one dissatisfied grumbler, or one peevish back-biter will work more harm, but for the same reason one strong man, one cheerful, ready worker can do more good, the more reason for cheerfulness, and to get back to Henry George, the less reason for individuals to believe the dismal prophets of today.

TWENTY YEARS IN FIGURES

Below are given some figures taken from Government reports that show the percentage of increase in some of our American industries in the last twenty years.

	Pct. Inc.
Area	5
Population	50
Wealth	121
Deposits in savings bank	180
Number of farms	44
Number engaged in agriculture	21
Value of farm products	70
Wool production	16
Wheat production	33
Corn production	94
Cotton production	56
Sugar production	308
Number mfg. establishments	100
Number of men employed in them	109

Now while these figures prove little in the case of manufacturers, because they may be controlled by central bodies or trusts, it does not show a great increase in individual wealth among farmers. For the farm still belongs to the individual, and he is the man who is least affected by monopoly and the movement for concentration of money power into a few hands.

FAIRS

This is the season of fairs, state fairs, county fairs, and little backwoods village fairs, and manufacturers, mindful of the customs of years, are packing up their goods and their samples and calling high-priced men off the road to go out and stand among the bewildered countrymen, cheap fakers—and, many times, insolent officials, in the dust and heat and rain, because—because why? Because their competitor will be there and they must not be outdone by a competitor.

Here is a suggestion. The next year, let your competitor go to the fairs. Take that money and the expenses and salary of that man or men, and get out a good, readable booklet. Make it the kind that tells your story in a simple, direct and heart to heart way. Send this out to the homes of farmers along about the first of November; catch him by his own fire in the evening with his soft shirt on. That is the time he goes through his mail. When the fire is acting good and the children are in bed, a pan of red apples on the table and the wife knitting, or singing a quiet little song in the kitchen. Just do this, that is to say, take him at this time, instead of going to the fairs, and see if you have not beaten your competitor's game to death. He won't be at the fair himself the year after; then the fairs will be left entirely to the faker, the man who gets the real good out of them.

1. In 1879 Robert Louis Stevenson crossed the United States to San Francisco. In one of the twelve essays in *Across the Plains* (1892), Stevenson described the American Midwest, saying of Nebraska: "It was a world almost without a feature; an empty sky, an empty earth; front and back, the line of railway stretched from horizon to horizon, like a cue across a billiard-board; on either hand, the green plain ran till it touched the skirts of heaven."

2. Henry George, known for the reformist economic policies proposed in his *Progress and Poverty* (1879), advocated confiscation of the "unearned increment" income of investors in land; otherwise, thought George, capitalism would not produce great wealth for the many.

Sherwood Anderson had to gain great pleasure from the appearance of his essays in Agricultural Advertising, *publications which would assure him friendly esteem from his colleagues in Chicago and some recognition from advertising officials across the nation. And the young author soon became understandably ambitious to write for a more general readership and to display his sophistication in subjects other than advertising. However he discovered* The Reader Illustrated Monthly Magazine, *begun in New York City in November of 1902 and soon transferred to Indianapolis, Indiana, where it was published by the Bobbs-Merrill Company, Anderson took advantage of its prestigious appearance and cosmopolitan contents to publish two essays (the second appeared in December 1903) on literature, essays which showed off smartly the breadth of reading that the small-town Ohio youth had mastered in and after his year of high-school education at Wittenberg Academy, along with some knowledge of the cultural and social events of 1903.*

15

A Business Man's Reading

The Reader 2 (October 1903): 503–04.

❧ *I meet often* enough such as you—bright, quick-minded fellows who, in a clash of wordy wits or a plunge into philosophy on a country road, are opponents worthy enough for any man. You go to the bottom of every truth; you catch every fleeting thought; you run swiftly ahead while we talk and build a breastwork of truth and logic, from behind which you rake us fore and aft when we come abreast. And then when we seek the storehouse from which you have so well filled your mental magazine, you promptly tell us that you are not readers; that you find Stevenson dull and Browning a bore; that you are business men and acquire your knowledge in the great human grind of the work, or in society if you happen to be of the petticoat faction.

Now, I have no quarrel with the statement that there is all the knowledge of a Solomon used in a wheat deal, nor that many writers are unspeakably dull. Neither do I expect Johnson or Williams to like what gives me joy. But I do quarrel with the way you approach reading and the end you think men seek.

To what purpose do you come to my room with your pipe when the lights are lit? You don't love me, surely, and I have no wife. Then, I conclude, because you storm up and down and look into my eyes and dig neck-breaking holes for me in the wilderness of argument, that you are here to whet your wit, to swing mental dumb-bells, and when the last pipe is lit and we are stripped for a finishing round, to knock me down and out with a storm of your best and strongest thoughts. And you had thought you could not fight with Stevenson nor take issue with Socrates? That Shakespeare spoke only the truth and Johnson was invincible? Where all that bravado with which you strutted away after your conquest of me? Where all that fire and logic? Here are fellows to shake you. Why not rush at Carlyle's conclusions as you did at mine? Lay a trap for Browning's unshaken faith. Say for me the things that Shakespeare neglected. Leave me at peace with my pipe and my book. The bookshelf is there.

I am told that the Women's Club of Ypsilanti, Michigan, will study Tennyson's *In Memoriam* this winter, and I suppose that all Ypsilanti women not in the club will have an uncomfortable time ere spring and golf, unless they, too, read hard of the English bard. Of course they won't all read and discuss to the end that they may quote, but many will, and those that do will sicken the heart of our clear-headed fellow of the street. They will quote to him over the cereal, and cut the morning orange with a sentence recommended in the critical introduction.

But you? Of course you will not be so absurd. You are a business man. You care not what Smith said when he had succeeded in merging the coffee-roasting interests. You wanted to know his plan, whether this or that move was good or bad; how he overcame this difficulty and how he avoided that sinkhole. You want the heart of the thing. Yes, but Tennyson was greater than Smith, and Emerson shrewder and clearer-headed than Jay Gould.

Go to them on the shelf there, and, forgetting the Women's Club and the school oration, read. If they convince you against your own judgment you had better look to your next deal in corn, or your late shipment to [the] Argentine. You were not so invincible then, were you? If you find there your own truths expressed better, ah, much better, than you or I can ever express them, read them, spend more time there and less time keeping me from my work. You will be a better man in the market place, and we shall smoke our pipes in peace.

16

Rot and Reason

Agricultural Advertising 10 (November 1903): 56, 58.

ABOUT COUNTRY ROADS

♔ *You can imagine* a fellow who spends his days in offices and his nights in all sorts of hotels looking forward with no little pleasure to a day on a country road among the farmers who buy the things he helps to advertise. When that fellow is fortunate enough to have for companion a man who understands the country and is full of a love of it and when these two start off at sunrise down a road that follows the winding course of the Mississippi and no more to carry than a stout stick for the chance of knocking down nuts from the trees along the road; when all of these things work out in this manner, I say, one fellow is rather bound to have a good day ahead of him. If you want to take part in a conversation that reaches every kind of business and life and is in a pleasant and happy vein withal, try this sort of walking on this sort of a day with this sort of a man. The road leads up hill and down, past farm houses and about sharp turns, over bridges and through marshes and along the road are many old companions of the catalogue and farm papers. Here is a wind mill and there a wire fence, here a cultivator and there a plow and up the road rolls the Studebaker wagon in use by the family going to church, and over all the quiet of Sunday and Indian summer.

ABOUT INQUIRIES

A western man, writing in the October issue of *Agricultural Advertising*, took up and discussed the old question of inquiries and whether it was better to use a paper that brought a few or many of them. He would have it supposed that it was a great merit to produce but few inquiries for the advertiser and argued quite eloquently to prove that the paper that constantly urged its readers to get in touch with advertisers was only paving the way to a large postage bill for that advertiser in sending out literature to curiosity seekers.[1]

I think that this argument would not go very far with many veterans in the mail order business. For the same reason that the retail merchant likes to see his store filled to overflowing with people, so the average advertiser is very glad to send his catalogue out in great numbers to such as will trouble to write for it. The retail man makes custom by getting people in to look at his goods, the mail order advertiser makes custom by getting his catalogue into the homes of the readers of farm papers. "Give me the inquiries and I will manage the sales," is the constant cry of the advertising manager of the country.

ABOUT CLEVERNESS

To be simply clever we would suppose to be a great thing. And certainly there are men who have done great things and made great reputations by pure cleverness. And yet cleverness won't win out without being backed up. It is like having a good cheiro. It must be a great satisfaction to be able to make a *b* that won't look like an *f*, or a *u* that won't show decided leanings toward an *n*, but after all, what's the use of writing well if you haven't anything to write? It's that way with cleverness. Mere superficial cleverness is of about as much value as a good hand with the pen. If you are a young fellow, you may be able to write fetching notes to the girls, and if you are clever they may call you cute and you will be a great hit in the high school and college clubs. I knew a fellow once who was cursed with this kind of cleverness. He was so confoundedly cute that after he had finished college, he began getting cute with the boss and jobs began to drop away from him so fast that he could not even remember all of the places he had graced with his cuteness.

In advertising, it wants a mixture of about eighty-five percent plain brains, then fifteen percent of cleverness and grace of expression, and the long clinging handshake helps out. It is said of a certain man in the East that he can buy a drink for a man with the best grace of any man in America, but what else can he do was asked. "O, not much of anything; keeps him busy buying drinks," or here's another: A western man, and a very successful one, remarked of his work: "I do not write ads; I sell them." That man ought to be of a great deal more value to his employers than a thousand clever men, but at the same time he would be of more value to his clients if he had that fifteen percent of ability to write a good copy. A well balanced man and the most valuable man is probably he who can not only express an idea and make it flower out into an advertising campaign, but who occasionally also gives birth to a brand new idea of his own.

ABOUT SUSPICION

A man has many things to bother him during any week of work, not least of these is the determination of one or two men among every dozen you meet who persist in believing that you have cards up your sleeve; that there is something about the advertising game that is settled behind closed doors and in mysterious whispers and a man must be foxy to win and then at night must lie and wonder if his neighbor has been even more foxy. There are stories told of how lawyers are constitutionally unfit to tell the truth; of how all politicians have their hands in the trousers pocket of the public. Would it not be better to believe that all lawyers and all politicians were honestly trying to benefit their clients than to believe that even one-half of them were grafters? For the same reason, I choose to believe that all men in the advertising business are really trying to do the square thing and help the man whose money they spend. Strange as it may seem, even our competitor may be a rather decent sort of fellow.

≈ Paragraphs

• No prophet is without honor if he talks of crop failures.

• The Chicago police recently picked up a Swedish woman on the street who knew not where she was going and whose English vocabulary consisted of but one word, "advertising."

• For many years now the American farmer has been making money and keeping a part of it. He's right.

• Did you ever stop to think that Marshall Field, one of the most dominant personalities of business, never has his face showing down from the dead walls or sensational columns of the daily papers and does not write articles on how to succeed for the magazines?

1. R. P. Fales, in "Inquiries Or Orders" in the October 1903 issue of *Agricultural Advertising*, had viewed advertisers' offers of free publicity materials as an appeal to greedy magazine readers rather than as an appeal to eager buyers of advertisers' goods.

17

Rot and Reason

Agricultural Advertising 10 (December 1903): 50–51.

THE OLD AND THE NEW

❧ *The everlasting effort* to say something new, or to say the old thing in a new way, leads to some strange freaks in this advertising business. To get this newness, men will sometimes sacrifice strength and utility and every other quality that makes for the one great end of all advertising; that is to say, to put money into the till. It is this everlasting effort for the new and the strange that leads to all the freakish, absurd stuff that sometimes appears in the street cars, magazines, and yes, even in the farm papers. The long-necked man with the one big ear, that appeared in the newspapers and street cars some time ago, is a type of this sort of thing, and a man who would use a thing so obnoxious does not stop to ask how it would affect him if put out by some other house. No, he is too intent upon eagerly thrusting it forward as something new. Men sometimes seem to forget that they are themselves the more easily convinced by well written, plain, excellent stuff that tells the story in an earnest, convincing way and then stops.

When Sol Smith Russell, the great American actor, died, men said of him: "He was an artist to his finger tips, and yet he made every part he played Sol Smith Russell." It is the best proof of a great painter that his work is so stamped with his individuality that he hardly needs to sign his name.[1]

Now, in the advertising business, when we speak of success, the word can mean but one thing. There is only one kind of business success, and that is the kind of success that makes money. The agricultural paper must make money for its advertisers, or it will lose them. The advertising man must make money for his house, or he loses his place. The advertising agency must make money for its clients, or it loses the clients. They will very soon go to some other house for their stuff. Therefore, it follows that if you, as an advertising agency, have made a success of your branch of the business, you have made your clients' business pay and you have succeeded that far. If you have done this for several people and have succeeded with all of them, one thing is sure. If your work bears a stamp of its own, if it can be picked up, mark this: it bears the stamp of individuality, because it is universally good. It has been tried. It wins.

There is one kind of advertising that is best for newspapers. There is another kind that is best for magazines, and still another kind that is best for farm papers. Do not try to switch the newspaper advertisement over into the farm paper. It don't pay. You are talking to another kind of man. What that man is and what he wants is known. How to tell him how to get what he wants is also known, that is to say, the way that will reach most of them.

Do not be led away by new schemes and amusing pictures when you want to sell a farmer a plow. As we said before, it won't pay.

A CHRISTMAS THOUGHT

There is a good, healthy sort of Christmas thought in certain recent developments in the business world. The country is awakening to the fact that the farmer, not Wall Street, rules the thing we call prosperity. Certain wise and far-seeing men have known this all the time, but most of us were not quite sure of it. Now all the daily newspapers are noting it with joy and surprise. Big reviews of weeklies are turning the gifted and analytical pens of their best contributors to bear upon the subject.

This country is like a great giant that has been told that a certain spot upon his body is vulnerable, that it is the keynote to his life, and when that has once been fairly struck by his old enemy Adversity, all is lost and he must go to ruin. "Behold," he now cries, "how foolish. The spot has been struck a vital blow and I am alive. I go about my business. I light fires in my furnaces. I eat. I sleep peacefully. How very foolish I have been. Now I shall not spend so much time and money and thought in protecting that one spot, but shall develop the whole and let it take its chances with the rest."

In the past, we have watched Wall Street and talked about the price of iron ruling the price of every commodity in the world. Shall we not now turn our eyes to the western wheat and corn fields and draw at least a part of our public confidence from them? We have surely thought enough about the stock markets. We have sent enough of our hard earned money there. In fact, in the past it is the money of the wheat fields which has gone into Wall Street life. Instead of putting this money into the development of manufacturing in the West, it has been sent East for investment on the stock exchange. We have been, in truth, very much in the position of that son of Italy who complained one frosty morning to a policeman, the while he looked ruefully at his frozen and ruined stock of fruit: "All of ze mon I make on ze peanut I lose on ze d-mn banan."

1. Anderson refers to the death in 1902 of Sol Smith Russell, American comic actor known for many performances since 1867.

18

The Man and the Book
The Reader 3 (December 1903): 71–73.

🐦 *We are told* by the learned and wise that the great mass of people who read at all, read only for the charm of the unravelled tale, and that the story with its little shivers of fear, its complications, and its heroine who goes bravely out into that boggy ground called matrimony, and thus out of the story, with her head tucked safely away on the broad shoulder of Sir Harold of Castlewood Hall, is the sort of thing most likely to run into the hundred thousands and build a country house for its author. "You must stop thinking and put your arms round William's neck," said a certain man of the world to a love-weary maiden, and to stop thinking and drag poor William down with the white arms of a woman is, we may suppose, the easiest way to the end and a certain name in the world.

These things may well be left to the authors, however, and surely they who feed us so generously should know what is best. At any rate, we may let the critics fight out their battles and turn to another fellow.

The man in the street—he who knows the unravelled tale in the sound of music from lighted houses at night, from lovers walking arm in arm in the park, and from wan, tired faces in the drift of the sidewalks—the man, in short, who, having much work to do in a short time, has learned the value of the hours given to reading and how to apply the good gleaned to the militant game of life as he plays it—this man, believing that the salvation of his soul can be worked out in the shoe business or the meat business or the hardware business, is apt to demand the kind of reading that will make him a better man in his work, and often falls into a habit of depending upon a few close friends among books.

I know a salesman for a wholesale grocery house who carried a volume of Macaulay's *Essays* in his hand-bag for years because he thought the reading of it on the trains and in the hotels at night helped him to sell soft sugar to Ohio grocery-men;[1] and, as one who keeps faith with a friend and is rewarded by finding the friend strong where he himself is weak, and hopeful where he is cast down, so I can imagine this fellow of sugar and side-meat turning in his hours of weakness to the strong logical mind of the lordly Macaulay for support. I'll warrant he found his Lordship sadly lacking many times; but where is he who has found a friend in the flesh who always feeds his hunger? And what a store of rich meaty sentences he had ever at hand, sentences that came back and said themselves over in his mind in the night time.

Take the case of young Billy Collins, the commercial artist. His friend and room-mate, Aldrich, guessed that knowing a few good books would awaken the sleeping ambition in Collins and make him produce better work. It began with leaving open books on the table and stopping a moment to cry their praises as Aldrich went out for the evening. This did not seem to work, and so Aldrich took to staying home of an evening and reading aloud. Collins was mightily bored, I'll tell you. He wanted to go and talk to the landlady's daughter. He didn't, though. He walked up and down, smoking his pipe and saying, "Hang the beastly old crew in your books." Aldrich went grimly on night after night, trying stories of adventure, Greek philosophers, biographies, everything, in fact, but stories with landladies' daughters in them. And then one night he found the thing that caught and held the heart of his friend and made him a reader of books, and finally an artist full of earnest love of his work. "The night Billy got the glory," Aldrich would say, lingering over the memory of it, "I wasn't trying for him at all. I just sat there reading alone. I'd lost hope in the dog, and didn't pay any attention when he came in and sat by the fire filling his pipe. It was Robert Louis [Stevenson] and 'Will o' the Mill,' and you know how a fellow loves to linger over the sentences and say them aloud.[2] It's like kissing a sweetheart. 'Why don't you read and not mumble that way?' he said, when he had filled his pipe. So I began and went through for him. When I had finished he asked me for the book, put it in his pocket and went out, and that night, after I had been abed for hours, I turned over and saw him sitting there by the fire, his face all lighted up and a look in his eye I hadn't seen before. I didn't say anything. I just rolled over and left him with Robert to watch the fish hanging in the current by the bridge and the people always going downward to the valley."

I might tell you of another case, of a friend of my own. A hot, strong-headed, silent man, from a family whose men had for generations burned the oil of life at a fierce blaze and gone to their deaths loved of women and with the names of bad men upon them. I can remember my own father telling of them and how they went their hot, handsome ways, careless and unafraid. This friend of mine was the son of one of the worst of these, but lived a quiet, sober, and useful life in the face of much head-shaking and wait-and-see talk among the wisest and best of our home folks. How grimly went the fight, and how in desperation he cast about for an outlet for the fierceness inside him, I knew. One day he came begging to go home for the evening, and when we had dined at a little place in Fourteenth Street we started home in the rain. I grumbled when he asked me to walk the two miles home, but finally consented, and we went off at a round pace. I was troubled about a piece of work on hand, and thought little of the man at my side, only to wonder at the way he covered ground, until as we turned for the last half mile the rain struck us in a wild flood and a fierce glad cry burst from the lips of him striding along, hat in hand, his big face thrust eagerly forward into the storm, the water dripping from his hair, and his eyes under the lights dancing with the excitement of it. Full of the old blood, I thought to myself and shuddered—a shudder that became a glow of admiration when at home over the fire he told me of the fight he had fought and how the battle went with him. Showed me his scars, poor devil, and then mended his battered armor with the man talk till morning. This is not a discussion of what is right or wrong for such a man. He had made a game fight, that is all we need to know, and when the lust of his fathers was strong on him and he was near to the sin he fought against, he would go into his room alone, and over and over repeat King Henry's cry to the English at Harfleur, "Once more unto the breach, dear friends!"[3] He told me that at such times he forgot even the meaning of the words on his lips, but that the rolling music of them soothed him and at last made him sleep unbeaten. And unbeaten he died, let me add for your curiosity's sake.

It is no difficult thing to find these instances of the way in which men call upon their friends among books in their hour of need. These few my eyes have seen, and only last week a young Chicagoan told me that the combination of words in the title "The Drums of the Fore and Aft" had come into his mind when he stood trembling outside an office where he had been sent with an important commission, and that they braced him and helped him to carry his plans through.[4] "And," he laughingly told me,"I never have read the story." Americans go naturally to their work like boys going to a foot-ball game, and, although they sometimes give their lives to the making of money, there is much of the music of words in them. Perhaps it is safe to say that in many instances their best work is done under the inspiration drawn from books, whose very titles are lost in the hurry and hubbub of their lives.

1. Thomas Babington Macaulay, English politician and author, was long admired for his intensely vivid essays, collected in 1843 in *Critical and Historical Essays*.

2. Collected in *The Merry Men and Other Tales* (1887), Stevenson's "Will o' the Mill" describes a miller tempted to wander from his native mountain valley downward to the plains below. Regarding the character's staying near his stream at home, Stevenson writes: "It sometimes made him glad when he noticed how the fishes kept their heads up stream. They, at least, stood faithfully by him, while all else were posting downward to the unknown world."

3. "Once more into the breach, dear friends, once more; / Or close the wall up with our English dead!"—Shakespeare, *Henry V* III. i. 1–2.

4. Rudyard Kipling, in *Drums of the Fore and Aft* (1898), describes two military boy-drummers, Lew and Jakin, both fourteen, who die ignorantly and uselessly in the cross-fire of an 1880 skirmish in Afghanistan.

As Sherwood Anderson began 1904, the fourth year of his work in advertising in Chicago, he conceived a new kind of essay for his welcomed contributions to Agricultural Advertising. *Surely without knowing of the Theophrastian "character" from the fourth century B.C. or its exem-*

plification in Renaissance France and England as the essay of generaliza-
tion that "types" or "typifies" human beings—Anderson in his ten"Business Types" caught the essential characteristics of various groups of people, not all of them types from the world of business and advertising but
from the whole rich society that Anderson had learned to study for the
telling detail, the vigorous mind-set, a knowledge of which would lead
him later, as a matured writer, into the understanding and describing, not
of the typical, the common, the ordinary, but instead of the more interesting opposite—the unusual, the unexpected in human personality, perhaps
even—someday—the "grotesque" character.

19

Business Types

Agricultural Advertising 11 (January 1904): 36.

THE GOOD FELLOW

❧ *He is probably* a fat man and it is sure he sleeps at night.
He doesn't always give you a contract and many, many times
he sends you away without even a promise, but there is something more than contracts and promises in this advertising
business, and sometimes an hour spent with the good fellow
will net you a dozen contracts in other places. The real good
fellow, like the real poet, is born, not made. His the pleasant,
ringing laugh, his the cheerful belief in other men's honesty
and good intent. Peace be to him and may his lines forever fall
in pleasant places.

He is interested in you and your lot. He has a few helpful
suggestions to smooth the road for you. He wants to make you
as happy, as good natured and as hopeful as himself, and he
usually succeeds.

Ben Yeager is a young fellow, just out of school, who becomes an advertising solicitor. Being quick, earnest and not
afraid of work, he is given a place in the western office of an

eastern farm paper. Just to break him in, and incidentally to get a lot of disagreeable work off his own hands, the boss sends him against the toughest games in the field. For weeks young Yeager beats the bushes, and starts no game. He hears rumors of business going out and daily he is told that there is business in the line he is working for a good man. "Stick to it, my boy. It will do you good, and don't be afraid to kick yourself. You probably need it." This is the half cynical advice of the boss. As though he wasn't sticking to it and fairly sweating blood in his effort to make good. He begins to lose faith in himself, to feel like a homeless little yellow dog. A grunted refusal is his lot in most places, and he has got so used to these refusals that he grows to expect them and can't for the life of him make a fight for business. And then he stumbles in on the good fellow.

The good fellow asks him to have a chair; he talks to him of crops and results; he makes the boy's heart jump by asking his advice about some matter of business policy. Young Yeager begins to feel like a man again. His knees go back into their places with a snap. He straightens his back. He begins to breathe again, the color comes back into his cheeks, his eyes glow, and he talks of that paper of his as he never had talked of it before. He talks as he used to talk up in the old college dormitory. He realizes that he is a man on the earth with other men; that he has a right to breathing room; to an opinion; to a place to work. He may get the good fellow's order or he may not, but he goes from the room a new man; a fellow to reckon with; a fellow who has proved himself.

Off with your hats then to this genial soul, he of the smile and the words of cheer, and may the advertising game yearly find in its ranks more of this good breed who are called good fellows, and are in reality only true born gentlemen after all.

20

Business Types

Agricultural Advertising 11 (February 1904): 19.

SILENT MEN

❧ *When Thomas Carlyle,* the growling Scotch philosopher of the North, had cursed to his full the Robespierres and Marats of France, he used to turn with something almost like love to ink in a passage to the glory of the silent man; the quiet man of work who with strong hands knew what to do and when to do it. We can imagine fine old Thomas coming to this part of his great work on a winter's evening when the fire burned and cheer sat on his heart.[1]

We are, ourselves, fond of supposing that in our day no such heroic treatment is necessary in discussing our own men and our own affairs; that, in fact, the Napoleons are dead and the world has settled down to mere buying and selling and the eating of three meals a day. This is but a pessimistic view of life and one not held with much favor among advertising men. They, who have seen their business grow up from nothing to a national power in a few years, know that the business life of a day in Chicago or Pittsburgh or Indianapolis or St. Paul holds its struggles and its victories great and small as in every day and every age in history. And as it was the silent, earnest men who gripped a mad world then and turned the fierce energies of a people to the orderly carrying of muskets, so now it is the silent man of the business firm who moves it with orderly force along the lines of success.

In every discussion of silent men it is only fair to say that they are of two distinct and widely varied types: the silent man of real power and the mere lout with no thought in him, who is silent because he has nothing to say. Let us not suppose that you and I, who are addicted to dabbling aimlessly [in] every subject under the sun, can by a New Year's resolution become silent and have in us the power of silence. As well say that by taking thought or eating a certain kind of breakfast food we could next week paint a great picture, write a poem or lead an army to victory.

Into the office of the silent man goes the solicitor. He is bubbling over with enthusiasm, full of talk, out to win his end. Now, the really fine man of silence, the kind we are talking about, doesn't discourage the solicitor or despise his eager enthusiasm. He likes it and he is ready to listen; but, as that solicitor hurries on from point to point, he begins gradually to talk less rapidly and carelessly; he begins to choose his words; for he realizes that this man knows his way through the woods and has in him a justice that weighs fairly. He finds himself saying fewer things and saying them better. Severe plainness in the ornaments of speech pays with this man and he, realizing this, omits many of his usual flourishes. In short, he feels the grip and power of the silent man, just as it is felt by all those about him; the same power that makes it possible for him to get things done without overmuch talking because his employees realize that they are working for a man.

The grafter, the fresh solicitor, or the empty-headed chatterbox will make but little progress with the silent man, for there is little gained by blowing with your breath against a stone wall. That sort of thing must be handled with a sledge hammer. When a man gets fresh, when he effervesces, or when he has cards up his sleeve, he would do better to give the silent man a wide berth, for his carelessly flung words will come home to roost and rankle in his bosom; and in the silence where only your own voice is heard it is uncomfortable to suddenly realize that the voice is not speaking the truth.

After all, there are a lot of really good reasons for the advertising manager keeping silent on most occasions and one who does this well and has in him a sense of humor must see sights and hear sounds, as a succession of good and bad solicitors plow past, to make food for much laughter. Blustering, pleading, whining, smiling, all are grist that come to his mill; and in the quiet evening, when men walk home from their day's work, if such an one cannot name over any wise or clever thing he has said during the working hours, he can at least chuckle cannily at the memory of fool things he has left unsaid.

1. In *The French Revolution*, completed in 1837, Carlyle claimed that, although the revolution had come as deserved punishment for the actions of foolish and selfish French nobles, extremist revolutionaries were totally abhorrent.

The revolutionary leader Robespierre, strong leader of the French Revolution, proponent of repression and execution of his enemies, was himself in 1794 executed by fellow-revolutionaries for his dictatorial actions.

Jean-Paul Marat, leader of the French Revolution who favored actions of vengeance against the nobility, died by assassination in 1793 because of revolutionary policy disagreements among the revolutionaries.

21

Business Types
Agricultural Advertising 11 (March 1904): 36–38.

THE MAN OF AFFAIRS

❧ *Peter Macveagh was* an Indiana boy who came up to Chicago to make his fortune. A clear-eyed, rosy-cheeked country boy, Peter was so healthy both in body and in mind that the whole world was a bright and cheerful place to him, and the winds that blew over the old farm had left in his soul no creepy dread or distrust of other humans to chill or dampen his fine ardor.

Down in Indiana on the farm Peter used to get out of bed every morning at daylight and go singing across the fields to the creek to wash the drowsiness all out of his body by a good plunge into the cold water. Then he would go back across the fields to the barn, clean the horses, milk the cows and eat his breakfast. After this, it was a straight stretch right through until night, plowing, seeding, hoeing, or some such work out in the open fields under the clear sky. Peter used to get covered with mud and he smelled rather badly of the stables at times, but under his rough clothes he was clean, right down through to his heart. It shone through the mud of the fields and the dust of the stables. It was in his fine eyes and his clear, red skin. He was like the fields and the woods, sort of kept clean by God and the seasons.

One day Peter packed up his little bundle of clothes and came to Chicago to live. He came because he wanted to mix with men and stretch his mental muscles. He rented a little back room on West Monroe Street and went to work in a downtown coal office.

Now in this house on West Monroe Street where Peter had come to live there lived, also, the usual assortment of Chicago boarding house people: Green, an assistant bookkeeper at the Corn Exchange; Miss Humphrey, a stenographer in the Fisher Building; Tomlinson, a shoe clerk; two medical students and a dentist with an office on Madison Street, and Peter's coming was woe to all of these.

Before coming to Chicago, Peter had had a talk with the old family minister down at home and as a result of that talk he had brought with him a box of good books, and being wide-awake and determined to advance, he intended to read those books. But work at the office was new to him and sitting at a desk very wearying to his active body, so that he found himself at night so tired and stupid that he couldn't read with an interest or beneficial result. "Well," said Peter, "then I'll read in the mornings."

So next morning when the shoe clerk and medical students and Miss Humphrey were deep in their morning slumber, they were awakened by a great splashing in the common bathroom in the center of the house. It was Peter washing his body awake for his morning hours of reading.

We will pass lightly over the events of the next three months. Peter was a human animal that washed himself, got up on Sunday morning, whistled in the halls, read Keats and Shakespeare aloud in a voice trained to call the cows, and truth is that Peter so shook up the dry bones in that boarding house that sad-eyed little Mrs. Thomas, the landlady, had to ask him to find another place. She didn't want to do it because she liked the boy and his habit of coming down into the kitchen and reading to her the while she cooked the breakfast. Then Peter had a way of making his own bed, and he swept and tidied his own room, and was very neat and careful about picking up his clothes; so that it was but little work for her to take care of him. But Mrs. Thomas was helplessly in the hands of the angry multitude, and Peter had to go.

Not that Peter cared. For his part he had been learning things these three months. First, he learned that the stories of financial influence, told at Mrs. Thomas' table by the assistant book-keeper, were mostly lies; that the medical students, who went off so fine in the morning with books under their arms, were not scholars and that they spent most of their evenings in Madison Street dance halls; and that for a fellow like himself, who really wanted to do good work, it was infinitely better to dine alone even at a cheap restaurant and enjoy the peace and comfort of silence, than to sit on Sundays and evenings in the gloomy silence among Mrs. Thomas' sleepy-faced boarders.

Of course, Peter was not settled in his mind about these people, but he went whistling about his work and thought of it only at odd moments. Slowly, however, the conviction began to creep in on him that in this world there are many people who are stupid and incompetent, and many more that are unclean pretenders. He wondered the more about this because of the miracles in the life about him and great forces that seemed to be always at work, moving the life of the city forward. As he went about his work on the street, and sometimes at his desk in the office at nights, he would pause and take in a quick breath at the wonder of it: the great, useful, massive buildings standing clean against the sky, the elevated trains with their loads of passengers; the great ships, unloading their cargoes in the man-made river. Everywhere was work getting itself done. Somewhere back of it all was another kind of man; his kind; clean, stout of heart, clear of mind, square and vigorous. When he passed a big office building, hurrying about his work as a solicitor (for Peter had been promoted), he would stop for a moment to feast his eye and say (with a little chuckle in his throat, as he passed on), "I wonder if that bookkeeper fellow built that." One evening, as he sat at his desk after the day's work, he decided to write to his friend, the old family minister down in Indiana, about it all. So he told him about the shoe clerk and the bank fellow and Miss Humphrey and the two medical students; of the drainage canal and of the buildings that sprang up in a night, and then he asked him the question: "Where are these other men; the men that do these things?"

The letter from his old friend was fine and fair and tempered with wisdom and much love for Peter. "Be fair with yourself, Peter," it said, "and don't worry about Mrs. Thomas' boarders. You are on the right track. Just keep on taking those 4:30 baths and reading your books; and when you can't understand a thing, whistle and wait. The men who made and are making Chicago were just the sort of boys you are, Peter, and after a time when you deserve to know these men, you will."

So Peter kept on at his work, and he grew; and he went forward; and he made money; and, by wisely investing it, became rich and in time was a very powerful man; but he was not the sort of man the Indiana minister intended; and for that matter, he was not the sort of man that young Peter had dreamed of when he was a solicitor for a coal office and walked the streets of Chicago. It were of little use to tell the story of Peter Macveagh and his affairs and end it here. To do so is only to repeat what has been said by dozens of men, and well said.

Articles have been written, and are being written every month, on the careers of such men as Peter. Their shrewdness, bold-ness and success have been bruited forth until our ears are filled with the din of it. But all of them go just as far with their man as I have gone with my Peter Macveagh, and then they drop him. He is clean, he is frugal, his morals are right, he has made money and, having made money, has succeeded is about the tone usually assumed by the scribe who tackles the prob-lem.

To us Americans this much seems to be taken for granted and the thought that Peter Macveagh (strong, rich and power-ful) may be a failure never seems to occur to us. We never dream of the possibility of his old friend and well-wisher (the family minister down in Indiana) having another sort of man in mind when he wrote his letter to Peter Macveagh. We lose sight of the fact that, in buckling down to his work and build-ing factories and getting away from Mrs. Thomas' boarders and forming trusts, Peter was doing about the simplest task there is to do: that is to say, about the simplest task for men like Peter. Here was a fellow of unusual vigor, and moral cleanli-ness, cast down among the hopeless ruck of folk who don't bathe more than once a week and are not thoroughly awake once in a year. How could he help getting rich? Or, for that matter, getting about anything else he might chance to want?

America is the sort of country that breeds strong men. It is rich with wonderful opportunities—opportunities that we, who walk in our sleep, don't see; and yet, in spite of the fact that it is a country for strong men, a really powerful man only appears in about the proportion of one to one hundred thou-sand of us common folks; and it is not to the glory of us who look up to such men, and who, by our praises, influence them in their desires that these men bend all of their powerful ener-gies to the acquisition of a few millions of dollars. In extenu-ation of such men and their lives, it is common for us to say that the strong men don't care for the money; that it is the power they seek; but, for my part, I am not able to see the distinction. The result to the man is exactly the same. Peter, grown in power, is not the Peter of old days; no more the good books nor the letters to his friend, the minister. He has learned the weaknesses of humanity now and is busy playing upon these weaknesses, and the blood that hurries through his brain draws warmth from his once big heart. Because he despises and sees the weaknesses of all men, all men hate and fear him, and he goes on his way, envied by no man except it be Green, the assistant bookkeeper, or the dentist on Madison Street. Peter Macveagh is a product of the times and the opportunities. His lust for power is satisfied because most of us are asleep. Mere living is so simple a matter for a man of average energy and intelligence that Peter, with no more effort comparatively, becomes rich and works his own ruin, for if we pay for our stupidity and drowsiness, Peter also pays for his title, Man of Affairs.

The "man of affairs" such as Peter Macveagh would recur in Anderson's fiction long after this 1903 story, especially in his novels Windy McPherson's Son *(1916),* Poor White *(1920),* Many Marriages *(1923) and* Dark Laughter *(1925)—all novels about American men who become all too easily successful in wealth and power but whose personalities become distorted by their devotion to securing these trappings of success in their nation. Sherwood Anderson himself really could have easily become wealthy and powerful in business; yet the cost to him, as he was eventually to realize (and always to remember), would be too high— the deformation of his personhood into grotesque unhappiness.*

22

Business Types

Agricultural Advertising 11 (April 1904): 39–40.

THE TRAVELING MAN

❧ *"Man," says the* poet, "is half divine," "and half asinine," replies the cynic. Now, I suppose the truth is that he is both of these and a lot of other unmentionable things besides. Of course the traveling man is only the average man away from home, and yet that somehow doesn't sound just true. He is a little more and less than that. Let's put it this way: He is the average man who has answered the wander call in his breast.

Were you ever a boy in a corn field on a hot June day, and just as you had come to the end of the row and were taking a long pull at the lukewarm water in the jug by the fence corner, did the afternoon train, westward bound at forty miles an hour, pass around the corner of the hill and go roaring and screaming off into the strange land that lay over and beyond Brownville? Or did this happen in the evening when you had washed the stains of the day's work from you and had gone down to the postoffice and then over to the depot to see the train go through? And did something give a savage tug at your heart so that it hurt, as with big hungry eyes you saw all of these people going so blandly and with such careless mien into that wonderful and enchanted land that lay east of Jasperville?

I know a fellow that has crept away by himself on many such a night and there, lying on his back amid the grass and looking at the stars, he had such a hungryness to get on that train that he thought he would die of it. Oh! to step briskly along as did that little round man with grip in his hand! To laugh and call by his first name the wonderful being with the brass buttons and the cap, and then to hear the bell ring, the snort of the engine and the plangent thump of the wheels upon the rails.

This boy that I remember had the thing all dreamed out. He would visit many strange cities, he would see the rivers and the hills and the vessels lying at their docks by the sea. And then he would make his fortune, by going to Cairo, Ill., and shining shoes. I have never heard of a man making his fortune by shining shoes at Cairo, Ill. I have heard it rumored, indeed, that the natives of those parts do not rise to the glories of polished shoes. But thus it was planned in the school map of his country and what cared he of the habits of the natives? In the barn there was even a box built to carry brushes and blacking, after the manner of the one slung so rakishly over the shoulder of orphan Harry in the Sunday-school leaflet. Cairo, land of promise, key of the Golden West: Why welcomed you not this youth, why sat you there idle?

But to our fellows of the grip: Hungry, lonely, story telling, hustling wanderers, outriders in the march of commerce. Yours is the grim duty of the scout. Well may you tell your stories. Well may you gather in crowds and with flaring song drink off your cup of fun. Loneliness sets on your heart and eats at the vitals of you, and you shall never inspan by the fire for the long days of home and home cooking.

Of course in this day all men travel—the manufacturer, the publisher, the professional man, the small merchant, the farmer, all have a grip stowed in the closet at home; all go forth to their schemes' ends. But what of them, what of the wife left three weeks in the year—only a vacation that, and good for the digestion, like an occasional physic. This is not the traveling man, nor is the son learning the business or the young genius working up the real thing. They are traveling incidentally. They don't "sell a line"; they are "pushing a proposition." The real thing knows the road and the trade first; he represents a business firm incidentally; he is doomed forever to uninteresting Saturday nights in lonely hotels a thousand miles from home.

And he is a very loose, big, hearty, tired fellow, who loves his wife and babies madly and is not always true to them. But we will leave this matter of his morals alone. Enough has been said on the subject, and why need we talk of it—we who are so pure?

About the best thing that can be said here about the old dyed-in-the-wool, six-months-twice-a-year traveling man, commonly called "one of the boys," is that he is passing. Modern methods, rapid transit, mails, electricity and advertising are sweeping the old ground away from under him. The winds of time will sweep the old boys into the past, and there will be new ones in their places, and that's fine. Fine for the hurrying, three-day-trip fellows who own their own airships; fine for business, fine for advertising, and finest of all for the wives and babes, who will then be able to keep tab on the goings and comings of daddy, and who knows, perhaps they can keep him straight.

While Sherwood Anderson was thus expressing pleasure at the disappearance of the traditional traveling salesman, with his rascality and his roguery, the young businessman was readying for a change in his own life, for he had fallen in love with Cornelia Platt Lane, daughter of a well-off manufacturer in Toledo, Ohio. College-educated, sophisticated, well-read, and traveled in Europe, Cornelia Lane, born in 1877 and one year younger than her new husband, brought to an already ambitious and prospering Sherwood Anderson the respectability and the responsibility of marriage, for their wedding took place in Toledo on May 16, 1904.

23

Business Types

Agricultural Advertising 11 (May 1904): 31–32.

THE UNDEVELOPED MAN

❧ *The advertising man* sat upon his upturned grip at a railroad junction. It was midnight, a drizzle of rain was in the air and close about him lay the unbroken blackness of a cloudy night.

Down the tracks in the railroad yards a freight engine was making up a train. The banging of the cars, the rumbling of the wheels, the swinging lanterns and the voices of the trainsmen lent interest to a long, dull wait. Suddenly up the track there came a rippling string of oaths, and for the next ten minutes the air was filled with them. In the words of Mark Twain, there was "swearing in that railroad yard, swearing that just laid over any swearing ever heard before."[1]

The engineer swore and he wasn't half bad; the conductor deftly caught up the refrain and embellished it, and then from far down in the yards the voice of a brakeman cut into the game.

It was all about a box car and a coupling pin that wouldn't catch, and it was nothing less than genius the way that brakeman handled his subject. He swore scientifically. He worked over the ground already covered by the engineer and conductor and from it harvested another crop, and then he caught his breath, waved his lantern and started into the dense forest of untried oaths. The best part of it all was the way he clung to that box car, he went far enough afield for words but when he used them they were pat, they were all descriptive of the car and its peculiar and general uselessness.

"He is a sort of genius in his way, ain't he?" said a weak, piping little voice at the advertising man's elbow. "He ought to be down in Texas punching cows. Take a feller with that kind of natural talent and he's simply being wasted working on a freight train. Why, the first thing he knows some mean, consumptive little town marshall'll come along and arrest him, and then where'll he be? Now take it down in Texas where there's a lot of room and breathing space and where it gets all still at night and a feller like that could do some fine work. I guess you don't know what I'm talking about. I seen you settin' here and you seemed kind-a interested, so I thought I'd come over and see you. I got a bunch of steers back here. Takin' 'em in. I'm a cow man, what you might call a cow man; not a rancher. I ain't none of these new business-man kind of a cow man that's cuttin' out all of the old ways. I'm just a little one doin' most of my own work and I guess that's why I'm so interested in that fellow down there. He don't mean no harm by that cussin', course he don't. It's kind-a like singin' to him and eases him off like. I've known hundreds of that kind in my day, the country down where I live used to be full of them. Trouble is they get so interested in their little old swearing that they ain't no good for anything else—they get so they do it for a stunt. It's like a feller I knew once in Arizona. He could imitate a jewsharp by puttin' his finger alongside his nose and blowing. He got so interested in it he couldn't hold a job. I guess it's so most anywhere. A feller gets so he can do some little fool thing pretty well and he becomes sort-a satisfied. Take that feller down there in the yards. I'll bet he wouldn't have that blamed proud ring in his voice that-a-way if he'd-a been where now and then he could hear some real swearin'.

"Say, young feller, you're different. What you so interested in that feller for?"

"Well, I'll tell you," said the advertising man. "I was just thinking what a good man he would be in the advertising business. He knows the value of words, that fellow does. Did you hear the way he made that conductor and that engineer look faded out like a scorched shirt front? He knows how to use words and that's why I think he'd make an advertising

man. How to use words, and say, Mr. Cowman, that's what
advertising is, just using words; just picking them out like that
fellow picked out his swear words and then dropping them
down in just the right place so they seem to mean something. I
don't want you to be making fun of that brakeman. You'll find
he's a long ways different man than that Arizona chap you tell
of imitating a jewsharp. He's a word man, that brakeman is,
and words are the greatest things ever invented.

"There's a lot of men can talk and talk, but that fellow didn't
waste a bit of his. He used just about two inches single column
on that box car, and you noticed she went where he wanted her
to go, didn't you? Of course, you don't know what I'm talking
about. But see here. You and I didn't see that brakeman at all,
did we? No, we just heard him swear and here we are, you and
I, quarreling about him. You want him to go down into Texas
to punch cows, but you're wrong. Down in that country there
won't anybody ever hear him except maybe a few scared
steers. Up in this country it's different. Why, there're millions
of people just waiting for someone to come along and develop
that brakeman. Say, I'll bet I could take him for six months and
have him making people believe I could pull their teeth by
mail. He's just pure waste now. He's an undeveloped advertising man, that's what that brakeman is.

"Well, here comes my train. Good night, Mr. Cowman. And
say, you leave that brakeman alone. Maybe he'll reform, go into
the advertising business, and quit wasting his talent on cuss
words."

1. In Chapter 6 of *Adventures of Huckleberry Finn* (1885), Twain describes Pap Finn's abilities in cursing: "Then the old man got to cussing,
and cussed everything and everybody he could think of, and then cussed
them all over again to make sure he hadn't skipped any, and after that he
polished off with a kind of a general cuss all round, including a consider-
able parcel of people which he didn't know the names of, and called them
what's-his-name, when he got to them, and went right along with his
cussing. " Later, after Pap Finn unwisely kicks a tub with his bare toes,
"the cussing he done then laid over anything he had ever done previous."

Having thus experimented with colloquial dialogue in a business essay, Sherwood Anderson attempted for Agricultural Advertising *a longer story that took advantage of his experiences in 1894 and 1895, when he worked in the first factory that came to his boyhood hometown of Clyde, Ohio—the manufacturer of the Elmore bicycle. Employing as many as one hundred workers, this factory provided young Anderson with his first awareness of the coming age of technology and his first observations of the deleterious effects of mechanization on the minds and bodies of factory workers. Yet such solemn contemplation would come to Anderson years later, long after this light-hearted discourse on manufacturing expertise and human nature.*

24

Business Types

Agricultural Advertising 11 (June 1904): 27–29.

THE LIAR—A VACATION STORY

❧ *They had met* by chance at the lake: the fish were not biting: the hotels were being filled rapidly with what the younger man called "a lot of Howard Chandler Christy people"; and their vacation wasn't more than half ended.[1] And so they bought them each a heavy blanket, to bear in a roll across the back, and, comforted by a vague belief that towns and occasional farm houses would provide them food and shelter on rainy nights, they started forth on a walking tour through Wisconsin.

There were six men in the party: a tall, lank, heavy jawed man, from his mannerisms evidently a lawyer; a dapper, nervous little man, with a red nose; a quiet bearded man; a minister, who had put away his broadcloth and his sermon voice for a month of freedom; a youth; and the liar.

When the party was making up, the liar had not been counted in. He was a new arrival at the lake and had no acquaintance among the five. He seemed, though, to give to each individual the impression that he was in some way very intimately acquainted with all of the other five. And so it came about that he was counted in.

It was agreed in the beginning, no man should reveal his identity or talk of business.

"We'll tramp, have some fun, say and do what we please, and then go on about our business," said the youth. "I hate this idea of making a little vacation together the excuse for reunions and all that sort of thing. If we don't happen to like each other overmuch at the end of the week, we can just drop each other, and there you are."

The thing worked beautifully the first day. They left the hotel at the day's beginning, and, laughing and talking, went in pairs along a shady road that wound in and out among the hills. At noon the little man with the red nose, who had been walking with the liar, shifted to the minister. He didn't say anything to betray his dissatisfaction at the result of his morning's walk, but during the long afternoon he occasionally looked back with something very like glee on his face to where the liar walked beside the man of law, who seemed oblivious to the glories of the afternoon, and only looked miserably toward the setting sun. After supper at a farm house, they went to a convenient hay loft for the night.

"We should have asked that fellow about the road for tomorrow," said the lawyer, as they stretched their legs upon the straw. "I think it would be as well to know at least the general directions: where the rivers are and things like that, you know."

"Oh! never mind that!" said the liar. "I know this country like a book."

The party looked at him with a show of surprise. The lawyer and the man with the red nose went to the top of the loft to sleep together.

It was the minister's turn the next day and he hung on like a dog till night. Truth is, he could do nothing else. At times there were none of the others in sight, and, when late in the afternoon they came upon red nose sitting under a tree, he refused to join them and hurried off after the bearded one.

The bearded man caught it the next morning, and the youth came in for his punishment in the afternoon.

That night in a little clump of trees above the river, five men sat about a camp fire. The liar had gone to the river for water. The young man got to his feet and said, with some show of warmth, "See, here! We've got to nail that fellow. He's a public pest. Anybody got a plan?" "Yes," said the minister, we've got to nail him down on something we know down to the ground. He won't talk about anything he thinks we're likely to know. I tried that. Why, say! he told me he was with Grant when he wrote his memoirs, and that he knew Teddy Roosevelt at Harvard." "It was Blaine with me," said the lawyer. "The way he laid out Blaine's private life was something horrible."[2]

"It was the inner secrets of Spanish politics he told me," said the red nosed one. "I never have wanted to fight with anyone so badly in my life. I'm going to do something if he isn't choked off."

"Let's get down to business," said the youngster, "he'll be back in a minute."

"Look here," said the bearded man, "I know about bicycles. I manufacture them. Let's see if we can land him there."

"All right," said the youngster, "that's a go. Here he comes."

When the liar got up to the fire he found the youngster, the red nose and the bearded man deep in a discussion of bicycles.

"I'll tell you it can't be done," said the bearded one. "There isn't a machine made that could spread the paint out over all of those little joints as smooth as that. No, sir, it can't be done."

"Well, a fellow told me," said the youth, "said he knew, said he worked in a bicycle factory once."

"I think it's done with some kind of a squirt gun," said the minister; "seems like I heard a story like that once. I've never been in a bicycle factory, however."

"What you fellows talking about?" cut in the liar.

"Oh! about bicycles: how they're made, and how the paint is put on," said the bearded man. "We were wondering if automobiles would ever be reduced in price as bicycles have been. The boy here says he talked to a fellow who worked in a shop where they were made. Says it's nearly all done by machinery. Says even the paint is put on by machinery. We don't happen to want to believe that, it's done so smooth and nice, you know."

"Oh, well," said the lawyer, "I don't suppose he knows anything about it."

"Let him tell what he knows. He may be able to set us all straight in the matter," said red nose.

"I guess you're about right there," said the liar; "I ought to know something about the business; I worked in a bicycle factory for three years. I guess I've done about everything there is to do about making bicycles. Why, say, look here, you fellows know who Col. Pope is, don't you? You don't? That's funny, why he's the biggest man in the bicycle business.[3] What's that got to do with it? I'm coming to that. Don't be in such an all-fired hurry. This Col. Pope's a friend of mine. No, he don't paint bicycles. Are you fellows all fools? You see, this Col. Pope and I started in business together and when it comes to the painting of bicycles I can tell you mighty quickly that you are all pretty wide of the mark. They aren't painted at all, you see. No, sir! it's enamel."

The four looked knowingly at each other and then settled down to take the full brunt of it. And they got it. The liar began with a long story of how be became interested in the bicycle business; he told of his father, and of his father's station in life; he recalled the days when bicycles were unknown, and touched on the old high wheels of his early manhood; and then dropping the autobiographic end of his little study, he conducted the party through a bicycle factory. He told of how the forgings entered the works, and wandered off into a little dissertation on tubing and the making of rubber tires. Then coming back to the work at hand, and surveying the party with the cocksure glitter in his eye that had so upset them on the road, he dived boldly into the inner workings of the bicycle business. He told of the filers and the polishers, of the blacksmiths and the assemblers, of the truers and the machinists, of gear and of crank hangers, of bearings and of handle bars, and then, after fifteen busy minutes in the enameling room, he closed with a short sermonette on prices and selling methods, yawned, knocked out his pipe, and with a proud look at the wondering faces of the five, he went off to the barn to sleep.

Four men sat silent before the dying fire. "Something tells me we've got it in the neck," said the youth.

"Can't you say something?" groaned the minister, looking at the bearded man.

"Oh! there's nothing to say," growled the manufacturer of bicycles. "He didn't leave one opening. He put every spoke in that wheel just where it belonged."

"What are we going to do?" asked the lawyer. "We'll have to believe every blamed lie he tells now."

"I know what I'm going to do," said red nose, "that fellow where we stopped for supper told me about a town five miles straight ahead down this road. I'm going there. Maybe I can catch a train to Chicago."

"Don't make so much noise," said the minister a few minutes later to the youth. "You can whistle when we get around that bend, not before. You don't want him to hear you now, with liberty just in sight, do you?"

In the barn the liar rolled over in the straw and went to sleep, with a satisfied grin upon his lips.

1. The popular and prolific nineteenth-century American genteel artist Howard Chandler Christy illustrated such sentimental works as collections of poetry by Henry Wadsworth Longfellow and James Whitcomb Riley; the aspect of his illustrations that irritated Anderson was the presentation of well-dressed, clean-cut, stereotypical American manhood and womanhood.

2. *The Personal Memoirs of U.S.Grant,* begun in 1884 and published in 1897, remains an admired example of American autobiography; James G. Blaine, Republican candidate for president in 1894, lost the election to Grover Cleveland, partly because of charges that Blaine was both unethical and untruthful.

3. In the early 1880s, the Pope Manufacturing Company developed and marketed the Columbia highwheel bicycle; beginning in 1888, the company manufactured the quite successful "safety" model of the Columbia bicycle.

25

Business Types
Agricultural Advertising 11 (July 1904): 43–44.

THE DISCOURAGED MAN

✿ *The discouraged man* stood in front of his place of business and looked at the buildings on the town's main street.

It was 1 o'clock of a hot summer's day and the only living thing in sight was a measly little yellow dog that wagged its tail at the discouraged man's side. Suddenly from around the corner there came a fat, bustling little man making a great fuss as he walked, and carrying in his hand a heavy grip. His straw hat was tilted well back on his head, and as he walked he smiled and talked aloud to himself.

The discouraged man put his thumb in his suspender strap and assumed a business-like attitude.

"Hello Adam," said the fat little man with the grip, "where's Eve?"

"She's dead," said the discouraged man, "everyone's dead, town's dead, country's dead, I'm dead. Wish I had the chunk of mud I was made from. I'd buy a big colored map of this state and plaster that mud all over these three counties so there wouldn't anyone remember such a place ever existed."

"Oh, you needn't worry," said the fat man, "most of them have forgotten it, I guess, even the railroad companies. But say, lock here! I have been in this town now twenty-four hours and I am an advertising man and an advertising man don't stay in any town twenty-four hours before something happens. You just come with me inside your place of business. I seem to feel a sort of hankering to start a little currency moving about [this] place. I believe in my soul that I am about to spend ten cents for a cigar."

"Now, look here, young fellow, don't you get me all excited and nervous about this thing and then go tapering off into stogies. I have been wanting to write a letter for three days to a brother of mine in Chicago. I want to ask him to lend me some money and the profit on the ten cent cigar will just pay the postage. Say, you might as well tell me any little bits of news you happen to have concealed on your person. The whole town'll be down to see you off tonight when the train goes and they'll find out about you, you can bet on that. This town's got a lot of enterprise that-a-way."

"Tell you! Why bless your old heart, Adam, you bet I'll tell you. Didn't I say I was an advertising man? I've been up to Brown's. Brown's the only wide-awake, up-to-date man your old town's got. Say Adam, the folks in this town don't appreciate Brown. He's all right. He makes the best all-around washing machine in the world and he had enterprise enough to write and get me to come up here. Say, does that letter you are going to send to your brother cost eight cents postage? If it does, just give it to me and let me carry it in my grip and you just push out a little better cigar. Thanks! That's better. Now, see here. You go get a pitcher of ice-water and towel and wrap up your head while I paint a little transformation scene for you.

"See that long, hot street out there? Not a living thing moving on it, is there? Well, she's going to be chuck full of teams just three weeks from now. Yes sir, teams pulling wagons loaded with Brown's Whirlwind Washer. The train's going to stop at this station four times a day. The postmaster's going to get his salary raised. The whole of this great, big, blooming, sun-kissed America's going to hear about Brown and his washing machine that is made right here in this town. The busy messenger boys will stop in front of your store to while away their spare moments tying cans to your dog's tail. The jocund automobile will whiz right past this very door. There will be the grinding of the wheels of commerce and the chug! chug! chug! of the gasoline engine stirring up soda water down in your basement.

"You're a discouraged man, I can see that plain enough. You have seen this town grow old and die and here you have been sitting for years, watching for some poor unsuspecting stranger to happen along and buy one of your ten-cent cigars so you could retire from the nerve-racking business life of this town.

"Well, here I come along, all unsuspected and unheralded, and bring the whole world to shop at your door and you don't even loosen up for a glass of lemonade. Thanks! that's not bad.

"Now, honest, man, I want to see you get right in this thing. Paint the front of your shop. Hire a good-looking lady cashier. Throw out those Louisiana Exposition cigars and get in line. You're living in Nearville, my man, Nearville the unknown and unheralded, the reticent, but, behold! a month passeth and the memory of man gladly forgets, and the Whirlwind Washer gets its picture in the newspapers from Maine to California.

"No, don't say anything; I see only too clearly what's going to happen. You're just going to sit here in the shop and see a great city growing up around you and you're not going to take notice until it is too late. You are a discouraged man. I know. I have seen them before. Poor chap! I am sorry. Just as likely as not you never will do any advertising yourself. Poor, poor old Adam! Well, remember me to Eve, when she wakes up in the cool of the afternoon. I will be gone then. Goodbye!

"Dang it! I wish I had landed Brown's contract. I hate to waste this whole day in this sleepy old town."

26

Business Types

Agricultural Advertising 11 (August 1904): 21–24.

THE SOLICITOR

✎ *The publisher of* the paper had often been heard to say that he didn't want an advertiser to keep on paying money to the *Farmer's Blast* who did not find that his advertising in that worthy organ paid. "However," he remarked, looking knowingly at this western representative, "we'll go on the principle of believing the *Blast* to be innocent until it's convicted and we'll let the advertiser hand down the judgment against us. We won't do it ourselves. It's like this in business," he went on. "We can't tell when an advertiser is going to strike oil. Why, when I was a bit younger, I used to be mighty proud when I told a man to stay out of my paper because it wouldn't pay him. Felt almost as good as I might have felt with his order in my pocket. You see I considered it sort of a moral victory, like paying a street car conductor when he has overlooked you, or returning an umbrella you've accidentally picked up in church. Well, as I was going to say, it went along until I found out that some of the fellows whom I had kind of looked down on as being robbers, because they took copy I had turned down, were around with testimonials telling how their paper had paid this same advertiser. Mind you, maybe the paper they had used wasn't any better medium for that particular advertiser than mine. Of course, I don't want you fellows to think I am looking for the earth, but I think you are badly mistaken about that Curtis-Crosby business and I don't think you need stay away from Curtis because of any qualms you may have on the score of the paper not paying him."

"Well, I don't know as we could get it anyway," said Bradley, the Western Manager. "The truth is, I've been over there and tried."

"Well now, that is something like," said the publisher, with a grin. "Why didn't you say that at first and not come in here with all that high-moral-plane talk? Of course, if you can't land him, you can't, I suppose, and there's an end of it. Just the same, I'm going over there to try it myself. You won't care, will you?"

"Care! No, I'll be delighted. Why, I talked three mortal hours to that fellow and never moved him. Then I made up my mind we didn't want it. I thought maybe I would sleep better if I looked at it that way."

A week later the publisher strolled into the Western Office of the paper.

"Say, Bradley," he remarked, lighting a cigar, "I've been down there to see Curtis. No, never mind about that, I can't stay. I'm just passing through, going back home, you see. Of course I'll tell you about it. I guess I've been thinking enough of it coming up on the train. Most of all, I've been thinking of how Curtis looked up and said 'goodbye' in that surly way of his. I guess, after all, you are right. We don't want that copy for the *Blast*. It might be wrong, morally wrong, you know, to take it. I wonder how you and I would feel if we saw a news item in the paper some morning that Curtis had murdered someone and was going to be hung. Say, I'll tell you what we'll do. We'll send the boy down there and let him tackle that fellow. He needs breaking in. I don't know any place where he can get more of it in fifteen minutes than by going down there and putting in that much time with Curtis after you and I have had it out with him."

The boy was a newcomer in the advertising field, a bright, young fellow, fresh from school, who was trying hard to break into the business. He had been dashing about for three months. It was hot summer and things were dull and the boy was discouraged.

"I don't seem to be able to line them up," he remarked to the Western Manager a few mornings later. "I guess I must be overlooking something."

"Oh, well! you needn't be discouraged," said the head of the office. "You've been after a lot of dead ones anyway. It's summer now and things are a bit dull. I suppose you'd better take a few days off and sort of take treatment for your nerve. But, say, look here. Here's something for you to do. Get on the train and go down here to Springfield. See Curtis, of the Curtis-Crosby Company. Get a thousand lines for the *Blast* from him. I don't know whether I ought to tell you, but this Curtis isn't a pleasant fellow. Fact is, he's sort of a terror. Look here, you go down there and land him. It means a raise in salary for you."

It was two days later and the boy was on the train bound for Springfield. He wasn't a bit deceived by the game to send him up against Curtis, though he hadn't said anything about it. In fact he had been watching the effort to capture that bit of business with no little interest and on the train that night as he lay in his berth, looking out at the fields, he was nervous, so nervous he couldn't sleep, and the worst part of it was he couldn't see any way out of it for him.

At Springfield the boy got up early and sat around the hotel, trying to think up some good plan. Then he went for a walk; walked around past the Curtis-Crosby plant; went back and got his breakfast; walked around past the plant again; went back and bought a cigar; and walked around again.

"Well," he said to himself, "this won't do. It's ten o'clock and I guess I better tackle it," so back he came again to the door of the Curtis-Crosby Company. "I'm getting acquainted on this street," he said to himself, with a nervous smile, as he went in at the door. "I reckon people along here are getting so they know me. I wonder if they think I'm in training."

Inside the office the boy received the message that he was to step right in with something like a shock; he hadn't expected that; he had expected to be kept waiting for at least an hour; he almost always had been even with what Bradley called the "dead ones." For all that he stepped bravely enough up to the desk.

"I am the boy," he said. "I am from the *Blast*. I am sent down here to try and get that thousand line order the other fellows couldn't get. I don't know what I'm going to say to you. I guess there isn't anything to say, but anyway, I would like to have the order."

Curtis looked up at him in a surprised manner a moment, then laughed and said, "You're a modest boy anyway, only asking for a thousand lines. Why, see here, I've got the order made out for five thousand. Here it is."

When the boy got back to the office, he started in to tell Bradley all about it, but Bradley only laughed and said, "You're altogether too modest, my boy," and so he got his salary raised and he got the name of being a good solicitor, which perhaps he was. At any rate, he is now, and that's all the story.

27

Business Types
Agricultural Advertising 11 (September 1904): 24–26.

THE HOT YOUNG 'UN AND THE COLD OLD 'UN

❧ *There were two* of them concerned in the matter, an old man, grown body-worn and watery about the eyes from hard service, and a young man not long out of the schools. The young man had the very best of chances for the place. He was a forceful young fellow with something clean and clear cut about him, and there wasn't a flaw in his business record. Bunker's big *Monthly* wanted a representative. The place offered a good salary and unusual chances for more in the future. Now, Bunker was not the kind of a man to take ahold of a thing and then let it go, and he had it figured out that this new

Monthly was going to be the best thing he had ever floated.

"It seems to take ahold with its teeth, don't it?" he said to the advertising manager. "If we can only get the right man for the West, now, we are fixed." This question of the right man for the western end had been hanging fire for three months, and Bunker felt that something ought to be done at once.

Young Cartwright's friends—and he had a lot of them— bold, clear-headed men of affairs—were ready to go far to back him. These friends were pulling every wire to land him in the place, and it was about settled in Bunker's mind that he should have it when a letter came in from the old man. It was a simple, straight-forward document, that letter from the old man, and it was something more than a business letter. "It's literature, that's what it is," said Wright, the editor. "You see he don't stick to dollars and cents and he don't tell what he has done, but he touches a fellow's heart, don't he? Better have him come up here, don't you think so?" "Have him up here? Well, I rather think so," said Bunker. "Tell you what I'll do: I'll have both of them up here next Saturday afternoon. We'll go down to that back room over the Mailing Department, and sit around the table. There'll be Wright, here, and Sutherland and myself, and I'll rig in two dummies just to add to the general impression of ponderous thought. I hate to say it, but you fellows don't give much of an impression of weight. You are both so thin about the legs and you haven't any place in particular where the bosom of a man's size shirt would lay flat, but I have got the boys in mind. One is a barber over on Fifteenth Street, and the other runs a tobacco store out in our suburb. I'll have them both put on their best black clothes and a strong, dignified expression, and then I'll lead these two men in and let them work out their own salvation. You fellows can do the talking, but I'll make them think the two broad-chested boys are the ones they must convince. I haven't told you, have I, that the tobacconist out in our suburb is as deaf as a post?"

It was Saturday afternoon, and five men sat by the table in the back room. Across from them sat the old man and young

Cartwright. Wright, the editor, was talking; the old man, apparently all unconscious of the weightiness of his words, was looking off across the housetops to where the lake lay, cool and green, with the cloud shadows fleeting across it. Cartwright sat up very straight and business-like in his chair. "You may consider it a bit unfair but this is rather an important thing to us— this choosing a western representative," said Wright. "The West is getting the business, just now, and we want a man out there who can go in and nail down a contract on the spot. We figure that the man who can come in here, this afternoon, and land this job, can go into other offices on other afternoons, and sell pages for *The Herald*. Mr. Cartwright, will you kindly arise and tell the gentlemen why you think you are the man for the place."

"And please speak right out, I'm a trifle deaf," said the tobacconist, who, born for director's duties, and compelled by fate to sell five-cent cigars to clerks having to catch morning trains, was feeling the importance of his newly acquired dignity. His silk hat lay before him on the table. His broad chest swelled with the importance of his mission. "Look at him," whispered Bunker to Wright. "He believes it himself. Looks a bit like the pictures of Napoleon at Austerlitz."[1]

The young man's voice, rising to a feverish pitch, cut the afternoon stillness of the building. It floated out on the afternoon breeze and some boys, playing at baseball in a vacant lot nearby, dropped their game and climbed upon a convenient fence to hear the speech. "I am not going to waste words, he began; I am here for business and I know you are. I have had four papers since I broke into the game out in the West, and I have smashed a record every time." (Here he looked over at the old man.) "I am young too," he went on, "young enough to say to you gentlemen that I can bring the best years of my life to you and to your proposition. I will work for it; I will lay awake nights for it; I will give my brains and my strength and my love to it; and I will make it go. I know I will make it go. I won't think of any other possible result. I believe I am the man for the place, and if you hire me I want you to know that I will be your man, body and soul."

He really said a lot more than this, but you have the meat of it. He grew excited, as he talked; he rose on his toes and pumped his arms up and down; he leaned far over the table toward the tobacconist, and looked deeply into his eyes. He was very much in earnest, was young Cartwright, and, as he talked, a smile played about the corners of the old man's mouth, but he kept his head resolutely turned to the open window.

"I am indeed sorry that one of you gentlemen cannot hear," said he in his turn. "But I am afraid I am a bit old to shout, and anyway I just rise to second this young gentleman's nomination. He says he will give his every pulsebeat to you and to your interests and you see I am a bit old to be so generous with my own blood and muscle. It's a good, long ways back to the time when I was a young man like that and hadn't made any failures and now you know I have made a lot of them, indeed I have, gentlemen. Nearly everything I have ever touched has slipped like water through my fingers, and then I couldn't possibly keep awake nights to think of you men and your business success. You're a very decent looking lot of men, but I don't know you and I hardly think I would ever get to know you so well but that I would want to forget you were alive in the evening when I got home and was sitting by my fireside. I wouldn't even want to realize that I had to work for you at all. When I wrote that letter I really thought I wanted this place and I came up here determined to go far to get it, but as I have been sitting here listening to this young man and thinking of the times when I have talked that way to men who were about to trust me with good places, something old and worn touched me on the arm, and out there and through the window and away over there by the lake I saw an empty bench by the park. I guess that is the place for me. But now I'm here and this young man has told you about himself, and what he is going to do for *The Herald*, I'm going to go over to the other side of the fence and tell you some things. I ought to be there, anyway. I ought to be sitting up there looking dignified and important and helping to hire a man for the place instead of standing over here on this side, an old man, asking for a chance to try again."

The tobacconist pushed his silk hat over to the side of his head, and caught his thumb in the arm-hole of his vest. Bunker leaned over the table and looked at the floor. Everyone else in the room was looking at the old man. "So here is my advice to you," he went on. "Hire this young man. You see that set look about the jaws, don't you? His hands you see grip the back of the chair." Young Cartwright arose and, ramming his hands deep into his pockets, walked to the window. "He is ready to do all he says he will do for you. He has a wife, possibly, but he will walk the floor at night thinking of schemes to advance your business. He has memories of the quiet days when he was a fellow in school, and wandered out in the woods in the summer afternoons and feasted his soul on a good book, but he has heard of other American hustlers who forewent everything pleasant and quiet and hammered through a long hot life on the trail of dollars and he is ready to do that for you. Gentlemen, it would be very foolish of you not to take him on."

The old man turned and went quietly out of the room. Young Cartwright followed as though he would speak to him. The barber and the tobacconist arose and put on their hats. "Here, you fellows stay and see this out," demanded Bunker, but they only shook their heads and went out without speaking.

"Well, what are you going to do," asked Wright. "Which man gets the place?" "Neither of those two," growled Bunker, "one is too hot, and the other is too blame cold!"

1. By his victory at the Battle of Austerlitz (2 December 1805), Napoleon forced Austria to make peace with France and kept Prussia from fighting him immediately.

28

Concerning Testimonials

Agricultural Advertising 11 (September 1904): 42–53.

⅋   *In the August* number of *Agricultural Advertising,* Mr. Kueckelhan, writing in the department called "Random Notes," gives us a vigorous and well-written exposition of the weak side of testimonials, attacking their effectiveness in advertising and in advertising literature.

It happens that we make our bread, and some little butter, by going up and down the land preaching the gospel of advertising, and particularly of agricultural advertising, and having had many good talks with the men who spend their money in advertising, regarding this same matter of the value of testimonials, we are moved to answer the gentleman with the Russian name. In this connection, we remember a talk we had one evening on the veranda of a little hotel down in Indiana, with one of the great old men of the advertising business. He was speaking of a brilliant young fellow who has recently shot athwart the advertising field.

"He's at the theoretical age," said this fine old man, pulling at his cigar.

"Most young fellows get that way some time in their career. They talk with half a dozen advertisers, and then go home and lay awake thinking of what they have heard. 'Eureka,' they cry, 'I have deducted this or that. It is evident that testimonials are no good, or that follow-up letters are a fraud. I shall here and now light the lamp, and sitting in my *robe de nuit* write articles for advertising magazines to prove that the things that were are no more.'"

We think the old man had got very near home. He had brought to light one of the weaknesses of any kind of writing on business, and on the advertising business in particular. Take the simple matter of testimonials and their value; tomes have been written to denounce them, and many a clever writer has tried in two pages to prove them absolutely of no account, but we can remember an advertiser who has another story to tell. We called on this man one day last summer. He had worked his inquiries with follow-up letters, booklets, and in every way known to clever advertising managers, and then as a last resort he sent out a big sheet of testimonials.

"I began to get orders then," he said. "Farmers seemed to like the idea of our telling them what other farmers thought of our goods."

Now, because certain manufacturers of proprietary medicines, consumption cures, cancer cures, and others of that ilk, and various floaters of investment schemes, have used testimonials that were evidently fraudulent, this writer in *Agricultural Advertising* asked us to throw this powerful agent for results overboard, and touch it no more with our fingers, because he says it is a thing unclean. How about good, plain, common sense in this matter? Are we to suppose that such advertisers as the Postum Cereal Company, Studebaker Bros. Mfg. Co., and other great and successful advertisers who use testimonials do not know what they are about? Or take this same number of *Agricultural Advertising,* and look to where one of the advertisers prints testimonials from such well-known houses as Montgomery Ward & Co., of Chicago; J. Stevens Arms and Tool Company of Chicopee Falls, Mass.; Kemp & Burpee of Syracuse, N.Y.; Kalamazoo Carriage & Harness Company of Kalamazoo, Mich.; and P. M. Sharples Company of West Chester, Pa.—are we to suppose such work ineffective and weak, and that these people could be induced to let their names appear at the bottom of an insincere testimonial? The simple truth is probably this: There are fools in the world in great numbers, but in the end at least a voting majority of the men and women who have money to spend are moved to their buying by good sense. These people will recognize a fraudulent testimonial, and they will be influenced by a straight, honest testimonial from an honest house published and put out by an honest advertiser. They will read it with interest because it is an expression of opinion by a man or firm of men who have spent good money to get the experience that is published broadcast. The gentleman who writes in *Agricultural Advertising* may have had quantities of insect powder offered him for his name at the bottom of a testimonial, but we will go the length of a good dinner he has had no offers of any kind from reputable advertisers for his name on a testimonial. Manufacturers of stoves, pianos, plows, wagons, and publishers of great periodicals do not buy testimonials, and do not need to buy testimonials. And all of these are constant and persistent users of testimonials in their advertising literature.

29

Business Types

Agricultural Advertising 11 (October 1904): 53.

THE BOYISH MAN

❧ *Ah, but it* is good to write of this man; and it is good for you, Mr. Reader, to stop in your day's work and think of him—the boyish man; the living man; the fellow with something refreshing about him; the fellow who, in the midst of life, when adversity calls hungry old shadows up before him, keeps in his heart a bit of his boyhood and on his lips a laugh at the grimness of the old world.

I met one of these fellows the other day. It was in a hot, crowded place, where two hundred people were striving all at once to alight from an incoming suburban train. A horrid, hot sun lay in the sky overhead, and men swore as the crowd jostled them back and forth, and, then, there was a cry from the crowd's edge, and in among us came, falling and crying out, the hurt form of a man; his head bleeding, his legs crumbling beneath him.

But let's go back to our story of the boyish man. I walked up with him from the train. He is a quiet fellow, a buyer for a big wholesale house, and usually when he talks to you it is with a sure, quiet tone with just a touch of boyish laughter mingled into his observation of men and life.

This morning his hands trembled and his lips moved as a woman's might in the presence of her dead.

"It hardly calls for that," I said. "We've got to expect that sort of thing. That's the way we pay for this big town of ours, and for our trains that carry us back and forth from the green, cool places where we live. It's pitiful, I know, but to make it a personal matter is hardly fair to the game of life as we play it."

"I know," he said. "And I dare say you're right, but I think you hardly see this thing as I do. I'm not thinking of that fellow at all. Say! When you were a little boy did you ever pretend you were two people? Well, I used to do that, and I've never got over the habit. Just now I'm that fellow's wife."

Once there was another fellow—a traveler. I've forgotten his name and it doesn't matter, anyway. He was just a fat, rosy-faced boy and he went to Africa to see what the land was like. They told him it could not be done, but he thought it could, and so he went ahead.

He traveled thousands of miles through the Black country where a white man had never set his foot before, and then he went up to London and told his story. Did they believe it? No! He was a rosy-faced boy and he laughed when he talked, and so the truth of his story was only admitted after other men had gone over his tracks with armies to back them up.

These two men are of the type I'm trying to write about—the men who laugh; the men who see life painted in the colors of boyhood. We have a lot of them in the advertising business. I think it's this kind of men that keep the game alive. The advertising business calls for unbounded hope, and it's only the boy among men who keeps hope ever in his heart. For when a man turns forty and there are a lot of raw places where his harness doesn't fit just right, it takes courage, boyishness and almost heroism to laugh and be a boy; but it's worth while—at least, for the rest of us.

As for the boy himself? Oh, that's another question. It is said of a certain wise Englishman that when his son came to him and announced that he was ready to go out into the world and tackle the game of life, he gave him this advice: "You are a very nice boy, but you are overmuch given to laughing. If you would succeed in life, you must be a solemn ass."

30

The Fussy Man and the Trimmer
Agricultural Advertising 11 (December 1904): 79, 81–82.

The Fussy Man: One Who Fusses
The Trimmer: One Who Cuts Things Out

❧ *I am writing* about the Fussy Man and the Trimmer, as applied to the advertising business, because this article is written for an advertising journal. As a matter of fact, you will find the Fussy Man and the Trimmer working side by side in any kind of business.

We all know the Fussy Man. He is the everlastingly busy man; he is so busy most of the time that he hasn't time to do anything; he will button-hole you and take a good hour of your time talking about a subject a thousand miles from the point; he will spin you a tale about how everlastingly busy he is, and how he is just driven to death with work; he will rush into this office and out of that room and, at the end of the day, he won't have done enough work to earn an honest cut of pie for a lazy beggar.

The other type of man, the Trimmer, works so noiselessly, so like a finely balanced machine, that we know but little of the great things he has done until he dies. Even his wife does not know about the work of the Trimmer, and the man who does not talk to his wife about his business, and the unfair way in which his employer treats him, is as much of a curiosity, in his way, as a toad at a live stock show.

The newspapers announce the death of the Trimmer. The little biographical sketch of him runs something like this:

"He was born in an Indiana village. His father, an honest blacksmith, dying early, left him with a living to make for his mother and some several small brothers and sisters, which living he made by taking hold very vigorously and earnestly as a clerk in the village store."

The newspaper biographer may go on to say he was a great church worker, but this does not always hold good as the Trimmer is sometimes a swearer of strong oaths and a teller of fearsome tales, but, in any event, the sketch will close with some such list of accomplishments as that the Trimmer has done a great amount of work as the head of a great business; he wrote a book on the history of the iron industry; he was an active member of ten clubs; he was a profound and consistent reader; he enjoyed fishing and golf; and he gave much time to his large family.

Such sketches of the lives of great Americans are become so common in the newspapers and the magazines that we pass them without comment, but if you think such men common in the daily walks and haunts of business, cast your eye about you and try to figure out how the record of the men about you would appear in print.

As I have been turning over the things I intended to say under the heading of the Fussy Man and the Trimmer, there has flashed into my mind a passage I remember to have read about an entirely different matter, and I have wondered if the Trimmer—the man who cuts out all the foolishness and gets things done—would not be found holding some such cynical opinion of us Fussy ones, could his opinion be had, which it can't, let us quickly add for the sake of our peace of mind. The passage goes something like this:

"For my part, I cannot think what the women mean. It might be very well if the Apollo Belvedere should suddenly glow all over into life, and step forward from the pedestal with that god-like air of his, but of the misbegotten changelings who call themselves men and prate intolerably over dinner tables, I never saw one who seemed worthy to inspire love."[1]

The other evening, after having dawdled through a long day, I sat in my train homeward bound and gave myself frankly over to remorse and shame because of the little I had that day accomplished. I had not hoped to do wonderful things, and I should have been satisfied to have written a few good, coaxing advertisements and thought out a plan or two for the advancement of some client's interests. "And," thought I, "this same train may well bear homeward some man who has today planned a great state movement, or finished an invention that will lighten the labor of a million hands. There he may be sitting among the row of men opposite me, thinking, not of what he [has] done, but planning other things to do while we Fussers go painfully over so small a matter as the making of our bread and butter, and wear ourselves into a state where we will end by being disagreeable to our wives!"

The train stopped, and I stepped down into the crisp air of a star-lit winter evening. The lights flashed among the penciled branches of the trees and into my befuddled brain there came a kind of answer to my questions. "The Trimmer," said the crisp night, "uses his brain. He is mentally busy. The rest of you work hard enough with your hands—altogether too hard; that is one of your troubles. You can't keep your hands off of things; you are so everlastingly busy doing things that don't need to be done, that you haven't time to do real work. Look at the common attitude of the president of almost any of your business institutions. The moment he sees a man sitting calmly looking out of a window, he jumps to the conclusion that the man is idling. It never occurs to him that the man may be working with his brain. The thing is so unusual that such an excuse offered to the average business man would be treated as an absurdity.

"No sir! You must be a fussy American. Get busy with your hands; walk feverishly up and down; swear when your train does not arrive, make a great show and bustle. You will be fussy and uncomfortable to live with and in the end you won't get much of anything done, but, at least, you won't get the reputation for being queer and indifferent and you won't get talked about in the newspapers and the magazines when you die. All of that sort of thing is for the Trimmer—the man who cuts things out."

"The night has, undoubtedly, taken a cynical turn," I thought as I fingered in the cold for the key-hole, "but it has given a kind of answer to my question as to the difference between the Trimmer and the Fussy Man."

1. Surviving only in copies, the most famous statue of the Greek god Apollo was probably sculpted by Leochares in the fourth century B.C.

Early in 1905, Sherwood Anderson and his writings on advertising and business came to the attention of a very important person—Cyrus Curtis, head of the Saturday Evening Post. *Having failed to meet Anderson at the advertising agency in Chicago, Curtis invited the young copywriter to submit for publication in the* Post *a story or essay based on business. The submitted work being for some reason unacceptable for publication, Curtis nevertheless arranged for Anderson to visit the company headquarters in Philadelphia. There is no clear explanation of why Curtis and Anderson did not agree on employment on the staff of the* Post, *but the recognition and the possibility of employment with such a huge company must have encouraged Anderson to consider other ways of improving his already comfortable financial and social situation. One result of such meditation on his future prospects brought from the young advertising man a proposal to improve his job as solicitor and writer of advertising copy by redefining the work into that of a professional management-consultant, available to any business needing sound service and willing to pay for such service in direct salary instead of in a percentage of advertising bought.*

31

The Sales Master and the Selling Organization

Agricultural Advertising 12 (April 1905): 306–08.

❧ *In America all* men are salesmen; at least all are salesmen whose eyes will fall upon this printed page. If you are not a salesman you are in some way concerned in the selling idea. You have dreamed your dream of the great selling organization you will create—how it shall be built, what sort of men shall command its positions, and how the organization shall storm the buying public. A moralized Standard Oil Company is the beau ideal of the average American business man.

And what a Chinese chop suey some of us make of our selling organizations! Every man must have his opinion to the front and then sit back to be admired. Beardless youths write strong sentences, print them on little colored placards and nail them about in offices, and the man who cannot "make good" in a $2000 position must write his book or pamphlet, setting down in serial rows all of the infallible precepts for building up a selling organization, like honest old Ben Franklin ruling his little note book that he might write down from day to day his inspired rules for living a perfect life.[1]

The great selling organization built on never so strong a foundation, honest goods and fair prices, has always this one element as a weakness—the stones that go to make up the great structure are human beings, and human beings do not stay in one place and do what they are told, no matter how many pamphlets you may write or how many placards you may stick on the wall behind their desks.

Why, I dare say, right here in this city on this cold March morning there are a thousand men sitting down at desks piled with unanswered letters and neglected work, and facing, meanwhile, that commanding and imperial placard, "Do It Now!"

The head of the sales department cannot make every one of the men that he sends out to do his bidding among the people who buy see the game as he sees it, and he will need much patience and a heart full of a great faith to get even a few of his salesmen to doing about what he believes is the right thing. The traveling man himself won't find the selling system always at his back, and every day there will be coming to the front cases where the whole carefully built-up system is only a hindrance, and he must strike out boldly in a new and untried field. And yet, in spite of all these things, the selling genius is coming into his own in this country.

This is evident in the pages of the magazines, where the old, cock-sure, "absolutely pure" advertiser is being replaced by the man who, in a clear, pleasing way, tells the people the "reason why."

The much-condemned mail order house has also been a factor, and in its own way has taught a grim lesson to the organization man. It has shown him many weak places in the old plan of pushing the goods into the hands of sleepy dealers, spending millions in declaring they are "absolutely pure," and then trusting to the inborn faith of the public to believe and buy. Note that the mail order house through their advertising began telling the people "why." The people like being told "why" and the mail order house prospered. Now the organization men are buying space in magazines and newspapers and are telling the people "why," and the people like that and will buy, and out of these conditions is arising an insistent demand for the selling genius, and the demand is not for the beardless youth writing placards, nor for the last summer graduate of a correspondence school which teaches you how it should be done in twenty printed lessons.

The man wanted is the salesman or advertising man who has had to sell goods for bread and butter, and who has kept his ear to the ground and probably a bunch of his competitors' advertisements stuck in every pocket of his coat.

The relation of the advertising agency man and the organization man is also changing. The ability to write good copy and buy space at low prices, which are and have been the chief claims to consideration of many a high priced agency man, are all right and very necessary. But with the growth of organizations and organization men there has come a demand for sound, practical business advice from the man who handles advertising.

There is a growing demand for the advertising man of a quick sympathy and appreciation of the ends sought by the sales manager; men who, because of their wide acquaintance-ship and their study of many problems, are able to keep the inside man alive to the other side of the story, and who help him to see the effects of his work upon the public.

Some years ago a number of young advertising men got together and talked these things over. They believed they could see in these conditions the possibilities of a great and needed profession, a profession that is day by day and year by year being more fully developed. These are the conditions that lay before the far-seeing eye of these men and pointed out to them the road they were trying to follow.

There are, in this country, many firms that, because of their size and limited capital, cannot afford a high-priced organization man to handle and develop new ideas for exploiting their goods; therefore the question arose, "Why should there not come from the ranks of American Advertising Men a class of business physicians who can walk into an office and lay their hands upon diseased spots in the selling system?" The requirements for such a position in the business world are many. Such a man would need to be—

First, absolutely unapproachable behind his fortification of business honor. He would need to be clean and with soul untainted by the lust of money, that he might not be swept aside by the many little opportunities for "graft" that would arise in his work. He would need to have in his heart a big love and pride in his profession, and he would need to be a quick and sure judge of human nature. You see, it is a sort of a compromise between the corporation lawyer and the advertising man that has been built up. Let us call him the Sales Master.

These men may, and probably will, in the scope of their work be carried far out beyond the present place of the advertising man. They will command fees magnificent, respect unlimited, honor among men. Certainly the conception is a noble one, and offers a working point worthy the effort of every sincere advertising man.

The sales masters in the business today are in the advertising agencies. It is no unusual thing for one of these men to not only see to it that his client is provided with good, strong copy for the advertisements themselves, but he prepares a good, strong follow-up system, his hand is felt in the formation of the selling arguments for the catalogue, and in many cases he enters into the formation of the selling organization itself, sometimes turning it completely around, and letting in new and helpful suggestions for the selling system.

And how is he paid for this work? By a commission on the advertising. That is to say, upon the amount of money spent. Are not the inconsistency of the position and the inadequacy of the compensation arrangement apparent? Why should such men be confined in their work to such firms as chance to be advertising in magazines, newspapers, street cars or bill boards?

No, the sales master has got to become a broader man than present conditions of the advertising agency will permit. He has got too much at stake, and the possibilities in the profession in fields out beyond are too alluring. Right here let me answer a question which may arise in the mind of some of my readers: "Why should not such a man as you describe go forthwith to a big corporation, prove his ability, and carry off a great prize in the way of a high-salaried position?"

Because, once employed by the great corporation, once

safely seated behind one of several desks with rows of commanding placards nailed on the wall behind, your sales master absolutely loses caste.

He is not, and can never be again the clear headed, wide awake outside man. In changing his position towards the selling system he becomes a part of it, and whereas the selling disease may lie at the very heart of the business, he, being employed with the functions of the lungs, cannot and will not see the wrong with his old, clear eye.

The sales master has got to work out his own salvation in another way. There will need to be first a re-adjustment of compensations. There will need to be an appreciation by the sales masters themselves that there can be many wonderfully successful selling campaigns laid out that do not and cannot include advertising under the ordinary accepted heads.

I believe the proposition will work out and that it will work out through the advertising agency. That, in fact, it is working out now. Men everywhere, here in Chicago, in New York, in Cincinnati, the whole country over, are groping about for their rightful places. This is apparent in literature sent out by advertising agencies, in which men honestly set down things they will seriously undertake to accomplish, in spite of the fact that the compensation arrangement cannot allow for any such work as they propose.

I here must undertake to set down as a maxim that—"No good business man can do more for you than you pay him for." (The sentence is not terse enough, and I foresee that it will not get itself printed on a placard.) But you will see the strength of it, that the advertising agency men of America cannot do the work that applies to the sales master on the same compensation arrangement that was in force fifteen years ago and is in force today.

Let me close my argument by predicting again that the sales master will get into his rightful place, and that when he does it will be the great much-needed healthy note in the advertising agency business. The advertising agency would then become really the agent of the advertiser and the agency business would go on in its growth until agency men are what we have called them in this article, sales masters, and the absurd plan of paying such a man a commission on his expenditure will be replaced by a system of compensation rated according to the service rendered.

1. In his *Autobiography,* Benjamin Franklin writes: "I conceived the bold and arduous project of arriving at moral perfection. I wished to live without committing any fault or crime; I would conquer all that either natural inclination, custom, or company might lead me into." To achieve such ultimate virtue, Franklin ruled his notebook into scheduled hours to be devoted to mastering each virtue in order.

32

Advertising a Nation
Agricultural Advertising 12 (May 1905): 389.

❧ *In some of* the older states of the Union, where civilization is supposed to have been carried to a higher and more perfect plane, there has developed a cynical type of man who gets his chief pleasure out of life by laughing at the pretensions and the advertising activities of such public men as President Roosevelt.[1]

The West and the doings of the West are a constant source of amusement to these men, and they kick up their heels with glee at the very mention of such names as Cleveland, Ohio; Wabash, Indiana; Omaha; and Dallas, Texas. These towns have recently been entertaining that most democratic of presidents, Theodore Roosevelt; and the man, coming among them with his clinched fist eloquence and his talk of the blessings of children, and his strong-headed belief in a square deal is—let us be thankful—not one of these cynical fellows who laugh.

Born amid the roar of Broadway, he is at home in the saddle out on the big prairie, and in the hills. He fits naturally into the life of the country where men are in the raw and know not the glories of the frock coat and the wrongs of the theatre trust.

There is no such man for appreciation of things as our President. He appreciated the West enough to go there and live during some of the formative years of his life. He appreciated the Spanish War enough to get out of it some of the warmest fighting it produced. He even appreciated the office of Vice-President and through it climbed to a presidency. Who shall say that such a man and such a President does not appreciate the advantages in the best sense? Let us hope we can say this without being misunderstood.

We believe that the dignity of the office this man fills is not injured by his appreciation of publicity. The man who cannot think of the word "Omaha" without a smile will probably chuckle over our own joy at this thought of the advertising ability of the President; but in our conception of the word, good advertising carries with it good goods, good intentions, making good; and if the present trip of the President or any of his impulsive actions of the past may be classed as advertising campaigns, he has at least carried with him the goods. He not only got the mountain lions he went after, but he got the good will of the people, all through the West, who heard him talk of the square deal; and he renewed again their faith in the good intentions of the government he represents.

And if within the past decade America has got into its rightful place in the councils of the nations, and has a great, new right to speak out its beliefs and its purposes, isn't it because we have had the right kind of advertising man to make for us our front before the world?

The first Roosevelt administration was an advertising campaign for the square deal. The people of America stood for the appropriation and followed it up with a new four years' contract for the big bodied, earnest man who engineered things. Who shall say we are, any of us, losers?

1. Theodore Roosevelt, who had in his youth lived in the Dakota Territory for two years, had published *Hunting Trips of a Ranchman* in 1885, *Ranch Life and the Hunting-Trail* in 1888, and the four-volume *Winning of the West*, 1889–96. As President, Roosevelt engaged wholeheartedly in implementing and expanding the conservation and national-parks policies of the Federal government.

With these comments on President Theodore Roosevelt and his nation in the summer of 1905, Sherwood Anderson gave up writing essays for Agricultural Advertising, *gave up publishing essays of any kind, and indeed gave up within a few months his career in advertising and his comfortable life in Chicago. In the autumn of 1906, age thirty, Anderson made a serious move to establish himself as an independent businessman, no longer dependent for his income on the commission system of advertising. Using contacts made as an advertising solicitor in Chicago, Anderson moved to Cleveland, Ohio, where he had been invited to become president of United Factories Company. As a chief executive officer, the ambitious young businessman was expected to use his expertise in promotions and sales to establish the mail-order company as a leading commercial enterprise.*

Outlet for several manufacturers, United Factories Company sold for its various makers such goods as roof-repair compound, heating stoves, poultry incubators, horse-drawn vehicles, house paints, and farming implements. There is every indication that Anderson worked hard to publicize and promote his new business; but fate was against him when some manufacturers provided him with inferior merchandise, losing the company thousands of dollars, and when the routine pressures of business administration proved either more bothersome or more distasteful than Anderson had expected.

Disappointed at his first failure as a businessman in Cleveland, Anderson yet chose to remain independent of the advertising-agency work that had earlier, for six years, supported him well in Chicago. By the autumn of 1907, the Anderson family (one son had been born in Cleveland) had moved to the small town of Elyria, Ohio, where, as head of the new Anderson Manufacturing Company, the entrepreneur could, with the aid of financial backers and his own unsecured promises, use his advertising skills to promote the mail-order sales of roof-repair compound, paints, varnishes, felt roofing materials, knives and scrapers, and perhaps "novelty items." Again, the Anderson company probably did not manu-

facture anything, instead repackaging and selling the goods produced by smaller factories—a practice of capitalism that would someday strike Anderson as peculiar and probably unethical. As the Andersons moved upward in society in Elyria, they belonged to the country club, where Anderson played golf with business associates; they attended meetings of a literary club, where new ideas adopted by the Andersons may have shocked their more conservative friends; they added a second son and a daughter to their family; and Anderson, by now a member of the Elks Club, extended his worldly goals into new business activities.

Along with his work as president of the Anderson Manufacturing Company, Sherwood became involved in a secondary enterprise—Commercial Democracy, a selling scheme with several investors as shareholders and the promise of stock in the company to cooperating dealers. Guaranteeing riches to retailers of roofing compounds, varnishes, shellacs, and similar chemical concoctions if the retailers would own shares of the corporation—known as the American Merchants Company—this organization was active by the autumn of 1911 and would continue for some months after its founder abandoned it in early 1913, while the separate Anderson Manufacturing Company would end with the dramatic departure of its unhappy president.

For Sherwood Anderson, in the midst of planning the making of money and the enjoyment of money, somehow became an unhappy, depressed businessman, probably within two years of his move to Elyria from Cleveland. Remembering the earlier pleasure at writing his essays and business stories in Chicago, the older Anderson let it be known in Elyria that, besides running his businesses, he was engaged in writing stories and novels that he intended to publish and which would make him famous as a creative artist. He showed versions of novels to business associates, his secretary typed drafts of at least two novels and several short stories, he appropriated for his literary study a room in the attic of his house, he submitted his writing for professional publication, and he slowly lost enthusiasm for the duties attendant on business and family. The psychological struggle that developed in the saddened and desperate businessman would become so momentous that resolution of the conflict would come only through the trauma of emotional collapse.

Whatever the oppressive and conflicting forces that drove Anderson to the mental disturbance that ended his career as business entrepreneur and conventional husband and father, his breakdown, late in November 1912, marked the turning point of his life—a turning away from the quest for money and social power and a turning toward the satisfaction of literary creation and social freedom. Murmuring about having wet feet from walking too long in a stream, Anderson strode out of the office of his fac-

tory in Elyria; and, three days later, after wandering about the wintry Ohio countryside in amnesia (or "fugue state") he was committed to a hospital in Cleveland. After several days of hospital treatment, Anderson regained the consciousness of his identity but not the strength or wish to resume his business and family obligations. Early in 1913, he left his wife and his children and his business associates and his investors and went back to Chicago, where, on this his third escape to that city, he would reshape his existence as a quest for inner happiness through art and beauty instead of a quest for the external pleasures that money and its attendant power could provide. At thirty-six, free at last to be poor and creative and content, Sherwood Anderson faced the adventure of the rest of his life.

It is likely that Sherwood Anderson had maintained contact with his business and advertising friends in Chicago during his years as entrepreneur in Ohio; and yet it must be a gauge of the quality of Anderson's advertising writing that, when he returned to Chicago early in 1913, he was able to resume his association with the Long-Critchfield Company as though he had been on a mere vacation from his desk. Back in advertising, Anderson wasted no time in asserting himself again as a theorist about the profession, for he immediately published two business essays in Agricultural Advertising—*an outlet for his writing in which his work had not appeared since May 1905.*

33

Making It Clear

Agricultural Advertising 24 (February 1913): 16.

❧ Dean Swift *never* printed one of his incisive cutting classics until it was all perfectly plain and clear to the servant girls in the house where he lived. Old Henry Fielding used to go down to the theatre after the play and gather together a bunch of the actors. Then he would be off to some coffee house and after putting ten or twelve long cool ones under his belt buckle would read them the latest thing he had written, watching their faces and listening to their comments as he read.[1] Either of these worthies would have made crackerjack writers of advertisements because they had a sense of the fact that good copy isn't good copy unless it gets across, unless it is perfectly clear to the most simple minded.

And making it clear doesn't consist of using one-syllable words nor looking all over the dictionary for children's expressions. It consists of knowing what you want to say and of saying it without getting yourself tangled up in a lot of inconsequential side issues that confuse and puzzle the mind.

Come right down to it, here is the proposition: Every man who makes anything for sale wants expression for his business. He may have manufacturing down pat, he may have a fine cost system and everything modern, efficient and high class throughout his offices and plant and if he hasn't found expression, or if he has misleading expression for his business, he is nowhere.

Advertising is Expression and that's all there is to advertising.

Did you ever see a bunch of kids go visiting? Two of them come into a house with their mother. They stand around and look at the kids in the house and their mother keeps talking and the kids get nowhere. Then first [thing] you know, they are out of the room with the home kids and have got together in their own way. The kid who can whip all the others has announced it and maybe got away with it. The kid whose father was in the war has put in his claim to distinction. They have all located themselves and got expressed.

There are a thousand makers of goods for which there is a market who are in the position those kids were in when they stood in the *front* room in the presence of their mothers. They haven't got themselves expressed; they are standing around self-conscious and worried and all fussed up and uncomfortable.

That's where the advertising man comes in. If he is a good one he takes those fellows out into the other room and tells them to spread around and enthuse and tell the facts about themselves and what they are making. And then he helps to find expression, helps them to tell their story to thousands as they would tell it to their personal friends.

When a proposition is well expressed the cards are on the table. If it's a good proposition it will win. If it isn't you'll lose.

1. Jonathan Swift, Dean of St. Patrick's Cathedral in Dublin, Ireland, wrote many essays satirizing English mistreatment of Irish citizens, as in *Drapier's Letters* (1724–35) and "A Modest Proposal" (1729).

Before gaining fame for his novels *Joseph Andrews* (1742) and *Tom Jones* (1749), Henry Fielding wrote twenty-five plays, mainly satires of politics in London in the 1730s.

34

The Badness Of Bad Advertising

Agricultural Advertising 24 (March 1913): 13.

❧ *Advertising consists of* making impressions. The clothes worn by a salesman, the appearance of a firm's salesrooms and offices, even the brand of cigars smoked by the company's officials is a part of the advertising policy of that firm.

Now the worst of bad advertising is not in its ineffectiveness but in just the fact that it is so devilish effective, and one piece of bad copy may set up in the mind of the public an impression that nothing on earth can efface.

There is a simple and tremendously effective method by which the advertiser may get this lesson for himself.

Most advertising, particularly publicity advertising, is fleeting. The public hurrying past gets an impression, a record is made on a thousand minds, a record quick, fleeting, but strangely indelible. It is as though you stood on the sidewalk while one after another cars loaded with people who looked at you through the car windows passed upon the street.

The next time you are on a street car think of this and for the moment fix your mind upon the scenes that pass before you.

A heavy red haired man is running along the sidewalk with a pipe in his mouth. A girl comes out of that corner house with a shawl about her head and with grease spots upon her kitchen dress. A man with a huge mouth throws back his head and laughs.

The car goes on. In your mind the red haired man is fixed as one who smokes a pipe as he runs, the girl as one who has grease spots on her dress, the man who laughs as one who has a huge mouth which he opens unnecessarily wide. Meet the red haired man and you will think of the pipe. See the young girl clad in furs coming out of the lobby of a theatre and your eyes instinctively search for the grease spots on her dress. Talk in your office to the man who laughed and you will not hear what he says because your mind is waiting for the huge mouth to fly open.

All the world's a stage, and all the men and women merely players is strikingly true of the advertiser when, for the moment, he lapses into bad copy.[1]

And the worst of the bad copy, like the bad acting, is not in its ineffectiveness but in its tremendous effectiveness in creating a wrong impression.

1. "All the world's a stage, / And all the men and women merely players."—Shakespeare, *As You Like It* II. vii. 139–40.

No matter how smoothly Sherwood Anderson resumed his work in Chicago as an advertising writer, both the city and the copywriter had changed greatly since his departure for Ohio in 1906. No longer would Anderson consider advertising his career; advertising was now and would remain merely a source of income for the physical necessities of his life—work that would be gladly abandoned as soon as his newly proclaimed literary ambitions became artistically and commercially viable. For Anderson had returned to Chicago as an author of important fiction, even if that fiction remained to be published.

And Chicago was agreeable to the would-be author. A change in the culture of the city had taken place in Anderson's six-year absence; now there were free-thinking, intellectually provocative friends to be found and cultivated and learned from. As a one-year high-school education at Wittenberg Academy had prepared a younger Sherwood Anderson for his entry into business success in Chicago in 1900, just so did acquaintance with the exciting individuals of the Chicago Renaissance prepare a middle-aged Anderson for the exciting if rigorous demands of serious literary authorship.

From around 1908 through World War I, Chicago unexpectedly claimed some of the most vital and innovative creative artists of the period. After the genteel literary realism exemplified by such writers as Robert Herrick, Henry Blake Fuller, Hamlin Garland, and William Vaughan Moody, Chicago had become favored with such exciting and liberated iconoclasts as Harriet Monroe, who in 1912 founded Poetry: A Magazine of Verse, destined to bring public recognition to Robert Frost, Ezra Pound, T. S. Eliot, W. B. Yeats, E. A. Robinson, Marianne Moore, Wallace Stevens, and William Carlos Williams; Maurice Browne, who in 1912 began the Chicago Little Theatre in order to perform drama by Ibsen, Strindberg, Wilde, Yeats, and Shaw; Francis Hackett, Floyd Dell, and Lucian Cary, who brought sophisticated book-reviewing to Chicago newspapers; Margaret Anderson, who in 1914 founded the Little Review in order to publish only the new writing that might excite her; and such startling new authors as Carl Sandburg, Edgar Lee Masters, Vachel Lindsay, and—eventually—Sherwood Anderson, who slowly found his entry into the literary groups of younger Chicago artists, bartering his story of escape from business into literature for admiration of his burning desire to publish great fiction. Anderson, cynically writing advertising by day to sustain his simple life and fervidly discussing freedom and creativity and beauty by night to sustain his new-found emotional life, tried to make for himself a new existence as one more of the self-proclaimed Bohemian Chicago children of the arts.

Yet, however well he profited from the criticism and the encouragement of his new Chicago friends and their openness to raw expression of life's literary truths, Anderson did not immediately rush to publish any of the stories or novels that he had brought from that mysterious attic study in his home in Elyria, Ohio. In fact, Anderson published nothing from March 1913 until March 1914, indicating that he was busy finding his way through the entanglements of his marriage responsibilities and the necessity of earning a living and into the clearing of personal space that would allow him to become a dedicated, full-time creative artist.

In one last attempt to knit together their troubled marriage, Sherwood and Cornelia Anderson and their three children lived in the winter of 1913–14 in a cabin in the Missouri Ozarks, Anderson hoping that one of his books, after revision, would soon be published to provide money for their living. Whatever novel or novels Anderson worked on in the wintry Missouri hills, no book by him was to appear as a result of this reclusive stay away from Chicago. The one important result of the months together for Sherwood and Cornelia was their decision that never again could they live together maritally, although neither felt an immediate need for divorce. When her husband returned to Chicago and his advertising work, Cornelia Anderson began training herself to become a public-school teacher—a profession that she followed for decades after her marriage with Sherwood Anderson.

Returned to his Chicago Renaissance friends, Anderson—romantically bearded and rustically dressed from his Ozark stay—immediately began writing again for the Little Review, *published by his friend (not relative) Margaret Anderson, and for* Agricultural Advertising, *the friendly editors of which again, after months without Anderson's presence in their company offices, accepted two of his business essays—the last such essays that Anderson would bother writing—for their June and August 1914 issues.*

35

The New Note

Little Review 1 (March 1914): 23.

✒ *The new note* in the craft of writing is in danger, as are all new and beautiful things born into the world, of being talked to death in the cradle. Already a cult of the new has sprung up, and doddering old fellows, yellow with their sins, run here and there crying out that they are true prophets of the new, just as, following last year's exhibit, every age-sick American painter began hastily to inject into his own work something clutched out of the seething mass of new forms and new effects scrawled upon the canvases by the living young cubists and futurists. Confused by the voices, they raised also their voices, multiplying the din. Forgetting the soul of the workman, they grasped at lines and solids, getting nothing.

In the trade of writing the so-called new note is as old as the world. Simply stated, it is a cry for the reinjection of truth and honesty into the craft; it is an appeal from the standards set up by money-making magazine and book publishers in Europe and America to the older, sweeter standards of the craft itself; it is the voice of the new man, come into a new world, proclaiming his right to speak out of the body and soul of youth, rather than through the bodies and souls of the master craftsmen who are gone.

In all the world there is no such thing as an old sunrise, an old wind upon the cheeks, or an old kiss from the lips of your beloved; and in the craft of writing there can be no such thing as age in the souls of the young poets and novelists who demand for themselves the right to stand up and be counted among the soldiers of the new. That there are such youths is brother to the fact that there are ardent young cubists and futurists, anarchists, socialists, and feminists; it is the promise of a perpetual sweet new birth of the world; it is as a strong wind come out of the virgin West.

One does not talk of his beloved even among the friends of his beloved; and so the talk of the new note in writing will be heard coming from the mouths of the aged and from the lips of oily ones who do not know of what they talk, but run about in circles, making noise and clamor. Do not be confused by them. They but follow the customs of their kind. They are the stript priests of the falling temples, piling stone on stone to build a new temple, that they may exact tribute as before.

Something has happened in the world of men. Old standards and old ideas tumble about our heads. In the dust and confusion of the falling of the timbers of the temple many voices are raised. Among the voices of the old priests who weep are raised also the voices of the many who cry, "Look at us! We are the new! We are the prophets; follow us!"

Something has happened in the world of men. Temples have been wrecked before only to be rebuilt, and destroying youth has danced only to become in turn a builder and in time a priest, muttering old words. Nothing in all of this new is new except this—that beside the youth dancing in the dust of the falling timbers is a maiden also dancing and proclaiming herself. "We will have a world not half but all new!" cry the youth and the maiden, dancing together.

Do not be led aside by the many voices crying of the new. Be ready to accept hardship for the sake of your craft in America—that is craft love.

36

More about the New Note

Little Review 1 (April 1914): 16–17.

❧ *The idea of* "the new note" might be worked out more fully, but after all little or nothing would be gained by elaboration. Given this note of craft love all the rest must follow, as the spirit of self-revelation, which is also a part of the new note, will follow any true present-day love of craft. You will remember we once discussed Conningsby Dawson's *The Garden without Walls.*[1] What I quarreled with in that book was that the writer looked outside of himself for his material. Even realists have done this—as, for example, Howells; and to that extent have failed. The master Zola failed here. Why do we so prize the work of Whitman, Tolstoy, Dostoevsky, Twain, and Fielding? Is it not because as we read we are constantly saying to ourselves, "This book is true. A man of flesh and blood like myself has lived the substance of it. In the love of his craft he has done the most difficult of all things: revealed the workings of his own soul and mind"?

To get near to the social advance for which all moderns hunger, is it not necessary to have first of all understanding? How can I love my neighbor if I do not understand him? And it is just in the wider diffusion of this understanding that the work of a great writer helps the advance of mankind. I would like to have you think much of this in your attitude toward all present-day writers. It is so easy for them to bluff us from our position, and I know from my own experience how baffling it is constantly to be coming upon good, well-done work that is false.

In this connection I am tempted to give you the substance of a formula I have just worked out. It lies here before me, and if you will accept it in the comradely spirit in which it is offered I shall be glad. It is the most delicate and the most unbelievably difficult task to catch, understand, and record your own mood. The thing must be done simply and without pretense or windiness, for the moment these creep in your record is no longer a record, but a mere mass of words meaning nothing. The value of such a record is not in the facts caught and recorded but in the fact of your having been able truthfully to make the record—something within yourself will tell you when you have not done it truthfully. I myself believe that when a man can thus stand aside from himself, recording simply and truthfully the inner workings of his own mind, he will be prepared to record truthfully the workings of other minds. In every man or woman dwell dozens of men and women, and the highly imaginative individual will lead fifty lives. Surely this can be said if it can be said that the unimaginative individual has led one life.

The practice of constantly and persistently making such a record as this will prove invaluable to the person who wishes to become a true critic of writing in the new spirit. Whenever he finds himself baffled in drawing a character or in judging one drawn by another, let him turn thus in upon himself, trusting with child-like simplicity and honesty the truth that lives in his own mind. Indeed, one of the great rewards of living with small children is to watch their faith in themselves and to try to emulate them in this art.

If the practice spoken of above is followed diligently, a kind of partnership will in time spring up between the hand and the brain of the writer. He will find himself becoming in truth a cattle herder, a drug clerk, a murderer, for the benefit of the hand that is writing of these, or the brain that is judging the work of another who has written of these.

To be sure this result will not always follow, and even after long and patient following of the system one will run into barren periods when the brain and the hand do not coordinate. In such a period it seems to me the part of wisdom to drop your work and begin again patiently making a record of the workings of your own mind, trying to put down truthfully those workings during the period of failure. I would like to scold everyone who writes, or who has to do with writing, into adopting this practice, which has been such a help and such a delight to me.

1. In his novel *The Garden without Walls* (1913), Conningsby Dawson creates a protagonist who, seeking "Heart's Desire," an unwalled garden, is tempted by three charming women. Appearing in a section of the *Little Review* called "Correspondence," Anderson's reference in "More About the New Note" to earlier "discussion" may be to a conversation with Margaret Anderson, editor of the periodical, for no earlier published reference by Anderson to this author and this novel has been located.

37

An Advertising Man in the Country

Agricultural Advertising 26 (June 1914): 41.

❧ *There is a* good deal of misunderstanding among city men in regard to the farmer. In some way the idea has grown up among us that the farmer of all people has been blessed of God. So often have we said to ourselves and to one another that the farmer is a lucky dog that in our minds his good fortune is exaggerated. We are half inclined to think of him as a kind of dilettante, riding to the fields in an automobile, drowsing away the day on the seat of a riding plow, punching the button that starts the machine that milks the cow, lying in the hammock and listening to the phonograph.

As a matter of fact the farmer is a laborer and only rises in dignity above the city laborer because his work takes him out of doors and because the master that drives him to toil is nature, not man.

And many farmers like many city men are not driven, they drift. Life among them is still on a low plane, books are rare, bathrooms uncommon and they do not as a class stand Doctor Johnson's test. They haven't good clothes to put on their backs nor good food to put into their mouths. "The poor man is a rascal," said Johnson, and by that test and after six months of life among farmers I declare him an immoral man—by the Johnson test.[1]

I did not come away from the country without a new respect for the publishers of farm papers. All my life I have heard these men talk of the difficulty of circulating their publications among the farmers and when I myself went into the country and found my farmer host receiving several farm papers and reading them eagerly, I was convinced that the publisher exaggerated the difficulty of his circulation problem.

Now the trouble with me as with all city men is just that I never went into the country until I went there to live. I did not see and did not know that the farmer still lives in a badly unventilated house, that he sleeps in his sweaty underwear, that he is many times not far beyond childhood in his mental development.

It is a fact worth considering that the country market for the real comforts of life, good clothing, underwear, furniture, cooking utensils, everything that makes life bearable in the modern city home, is unlimited.

My own thought is that general advertisers should invade more persistently the agricultural field, that they should support the agricultural press in its effort to lead the farmer along the road toward culture and the impulse toward decent living. A general movement toward the wider use of farm papers for advertising the ordinary comforts of life will do more than can any government commission to better conditions for those dwellers in the lonely farmhouse on the side road, the farmer and the farmer's wife. Using Dr. Johnson's test again, it will do more than anything else can do to make the farmer a cleaner, better, more intelligent farmer. It will help make him a moral man.

In the matter of copy it is in my mind that it would be well for every copy writer to forget as far as it lies in the city man to forget the "Nature's Nobleman" version of the farmer. Let's be simple and plain as children talking to children. It will win. It will do more than anything else to help our advertisers get their story across to the man in the country, the man who after all is a child with the mind of a child.

1. This quotation from the eighteenth-century wit has not been located. The closest reference is "Every poor man is a fool," from James Howell's *Proverbs* (1659).

Easily the most unexpected publication by Sherwood Anderson in his years of apprentice fiction-writing appeared in the July 1914 issue of that most respected of all "establishment" American periodicals—Harper's Monthly Magazine. Founded in 1850, Harper's had appealed to readers with such contributors as Herman Melville, Henry James, William Dean Howells, Hamlin Garland, Sara Orne Jewett, Mark Twain, Theodore Roosevelt, and Woodrow Wilson. Harper's "Easy Chair" column, conducted from 1901 to 1920 by William Dean Howells, had led in the formation of genteel, middle-brow American literary taste; and its editor from 1869 to 1919, Henry M. Alden, had done little to advance the cause of the shocking new crudity in American fiction which such free minds as Sherwood Anderson were championing.

There is some possibility that Anderson had written "The Rabbit-Pen" while he was a businessman in Elyria, Ohio, and that word of the acceptance of the story by Harper's reached the distracted patient as he recovered from amnesia or fugue state in a Cleveland hospital late in November 1912. There is, likewise, probably some truth to Anderson's claim that he wrote the story in response to a challenge to his stout declaration that William Dean Howells and his crowd of tame Harper's writers could not handle the so-called base and vulgar aspects of sex and birth and death—the real emotions worth writing about. Challenged to prove his ability to equal or surpass the polite realism of Howells, Anderson created a tale of animal violence and human frustration.

38

The Rabbit-Pen

Harper's 129 (July 1914): 207–10.

✺ *In a wire* pen beside the gravel path, Fordyce, walking in the garden of his friend Harkness and imagining marriage, came upon a tragedy. A litter of new-born rabbits lay upon the straw scattered about the pen. They were blind; they were hairless; they were blue-black of body; they oscillated their heads in mute appeal. In the center of the pen lay one of the tiny things, dead. Above the little dead body a struggle went on.

The mother rabbit fought the father furiously. A wild fire was in her eyes. She rushed at the huge fellow again and again.

The man who had written two successful novels stood trembling in the path. He saw the father rabbit and the furious little mother struggling in the midst of the new life scattered about the pen, and his hands shook and his lips grew white. He was afraid that the mother of the litter would be killed in the struggle. A cry of sympathy broke from his lips. "Help here! Help! There is murder being done!" he shouted.

Out at the back door of the house came Gretchen, the housekeeper. She ran rapidly down the gravel path. Seeing the struggle going on in the wire pen, she knelt, and, tearing open a little door, dragged the father rabbit out of the pen. In her strong grasp the father rabbit hung by his ears, huge and grotesque. He kicked out with his heels. Turning, she flung him through an open window into a child's play-house standing amid the shrubbery beside the path.

Fordyce stood in the path, looking at the little dead rabbit in the center of the pen. He thought that it should be taken away, and wondered how it might be done. He tried to think of himself reaching through the little door into the cage and taking the little blue-black dead thing into his hand; but the housekeeper, coming from the child's play-house with a child's shovel in her hand, reached into the pen and threw the body over the shrubbery into the vegetable-garden beyond.

Fordyce followed her—the free-walking, straight-backed Gretchen—into the stable at the end of the gravel path. He heard her talking, in her bold, quick way, to Hans, the stableman. He wondered what she was saying that made Hans smile. He sat on a chair by the stable door, watching her as she walked back to the house.

Hans, the stableman, finished the righting of things in the home of the rabbits. The tragedy was effaced; the dead rabbit buried among the cabbages in the garden. Into the wire pen Hans put fresh, new straw. Fordyce wondered what Gretchen had said to Hans in that language. He was overcome by her efficiency. "She knew what to do, and yet, no doubt, like me, she knew nothing of rabbits," he thought, lost in wonder.

Hans came back into the stable and began again polishing the trimmings of a harness hanging on the wall. "He was trying to kill the young males," he explained in broken English.

Fordyce told Harkness of the affair of the rabbit-pen. "She was magnificent," he said. "She saved all of that new life while I stood by, trembling and impotent. I went up to my room and sat thinking of her. She should be spending her days caring for new life, making it fine and purposeful, and not be counting sheets and wrangling with the iceman for an old, worn-out newspaper hack like you."

Joe Harkness had laughed. "Same old sentimental, susceptible Frank," he had shouted, joyously. "Romancing about every woman you see, but keeping well clear of them, just the same."

Sitting on the wide veranda in the late afternoon, Fordyce read a book. He was alone, so it was his own book. As he read, he wondered that so many thousands of people had failed to buy and appreciate it. Between paragraphs he became entangled in one of his own fancies—the charming fancies that never became realities. He imagined himself the proud husband of Gretchen, the housekeeper.

Fordyce was always being a proud husband. Scarcely a week passed without the experience. It was satisfying and complete. He felt now that he had never been prouder husband to a more beautiful or more capable woman than Gretchen. Gretchen was complete. She was a Brunhilde. Her fine face, crowned by thick, smooth hair, and her quiet, efficient manner, brought a thrill of pride. He saw himself getting off the train in the evening at some Chicago suburb and walking through the shady streets to the frame house where Gretchen waited at the door.

Glancing up, his eyes rested on the wide emerald lawn. In the shrubbery, Hans, the stableman, worked with a pair of pruning-shears. Fordyce began thinking of the master of the house and its mistress, Ruth—the brown-eyed, soft-voiced Ruth with the boyish freckles. Joe, comrade of the struggling newspaper days, was married to pretty Ruth and her fortune, and went off to meetings of directors in the city, as he had gone this afternoon. "Good old Joe," thought Fordyce, with a wave of tenderness. "For him no more uncertainties, no more heart-aches."

From the nursery at the top of the house came the petulant voices of the children. They were refusing to be off to bed at the command of their mother, refusing to be quiet, as they had been refusing her commands all afternoon. They romped and shouted in the nursery, throwing things about. Fordyce could hear the clear, argumentative voice of the older boy.

"Don't be obstinate, mother," said the boy; "we will be quiet after a while."

The man sitting on the veranda could picture the gentle mother. She would be standing in the doorway of the nursery—the beautiful children's room with the pictures of ships on the walls—and there would be the vague, baffled, uncertain look in her eyes. She would be trying to make herself severe and commanding, and the children would be defying her. The listening man closed his book with a bang. A shiver of impatience ran through him. "Damn!" he said, swiftly. "Damn!"

From below-stairs came the sharp, clicking sound of footsteps. A voice, firm and purposeful, called up to the nursery. "*Schweig,*" commanded the voice of Gretchen, the housekeeper.

Above-stairs all became quiet. The mother, coming slowly down, joined Fordyce on the veranda. They sat together discussing books. They talked of the work of educators among children.

"I can do nothing with my own children," said Ruth Harkness. "They look to that Gretchen for everything."

In the house Fordyce could hear the housekeeper moving about, up and down the stairs, and in and out of the living-room; he could see her through the windows and the open doors. She went about silently, putting the house in order. Above in the nursery all was peace and quiet.

Fordyce stayed on as a guest at Cottesbrooke, finishing his third book. With him stayed Gretchen, putting the house in order for the winter; Harkness, with Ruth, the two boys and the servants, had gone to the city home. It was autumn, and the brown leaves went dancing through the bare shrubbery on the lawn. In his overcoat Frank now sat on the veranda and looked at the hurrying leaves. He was being one of the leaves.

"I am dead and brown and without care, and that is I now being blown by the wind across the dead grass," he told himself.

At the end of the veranda, near the carriage entrance, stood his trunk. His brown bag was by his feet.

Out through the door of the house came Gretchen. She stood by the railing at the edge of the veranda, talking. "I am not satisfied with this family," she said. "I shall be leaving them. There is too much money."

She turned, waving her hand and talking vehemently. "It is of no account to save," she declared. "I am best at the saving. In this house all summer I have made the butter for the table from cream that has spoiled. Things were wasted in the kitchen and I have stopped that. It has passed unnoticed. I know every sheet, every towel. Is it appreciated? Master Harkness and mistress—they do not know that I know, and do not care. The sour cream they would see thrown to the pig. Uh!— It is no use to be saving here."

Fordyce thought that he was near to being a real husband. It came into his mind to spring from his chair and beseech this frugal woman to come and save the soured cream in a frame house in a Chicago suburb. While he hesitated, she turned and disappeared into the house. *"Auf Wiedersehen!"* she called to him over her shoulder.

He went along the veranda and climbed into the carriage. He went slowly, looking back at the door through which she had disappeared. He was thinking of the day in the green summer when he had stood in the gravel path by the wire rabbit-pen, watching her straighten out the affair in the family of the rabbits. As on that day, he now felt strangely impotent and incapable. "I should be taking things into my own hands," he reflected, while Hans drove the carriage along the road under the bare trees.

Now it was February, with the snow lying piled along the edges of the city streets. Sitting in the office of his friend Harkness, Fordyce, looking through the window, could see the lake, blue and cold and lonely.

Fordyce turned from the window to his friend, at work among the letters on the desk. "It is of no avail to look sternly and forbiddingly at me," he said. "I will not go away. I have sold the book I wrote at your house, and have money in my pocket. Now I will take you to dine with me, and after the dinner I will get on a train and start on a trip to Germany. There is a reason why I should learn to speak the German language. I hear housekeepers talking to stablemen about the doings of rabbits in pens, and it gets into my mind that I don't know what they say. They may whisper secrets of life in that language. I have a wish to know everything, and I shall begin by knowing the German language. Perhaps I shall get me a wife over there and come home a proud and serious husband. It would be policy for you to drop letter-signing and come to dine with me while yet I am a free man."

In the restaurant they had come to the cigars, and Harkness was talking of life in his house. He was talking intimately, as a man talks only to one who is near and dear to him.

"I have been unhappy," said Harkness. "A struggle has gone on in which I have lost."

His friend said nothing. Putting down his cigar, he fingered the thin stem of the glass that sat before him.

"In Germany I engaged Gretchen," said Harkness, talking rapidly. "I got her for the management of our house and for the boys. They were unruly, and Ruth could do nothing with them. Also we thought it would be well for them to know the German language.

"In our house, after we got Gretchen, peace came. The boys stayed diligently at their lessons. When in the schoolroom at the top of the house they were unruly, Gretchen came to the foot of the stairs, '*Schweig*,' she shouted, and they were intent upon their lessons.

"In the house Gretchen went about quietly. She did the work of the house thoroughly. When I came home in the evening the toys of the children no longer were scattered about underfoot. They were gathered into the boxes put into the nursery for the purpose.

"Our two boys sat quietly with us at the evening meal. When they had been well-mannered they looked for approval to Gretchen, who talked to them in German. Ruth did not speak German. She sat at the table, looking at the boys and at Gretchen. She was unhappy in her own home, but I did not know why.

"One evening when the boys had gone up-stairs with Gretchen she turned to me, saying intensely, 'I hate German!' I thought her over-tired. 'You should see a physician for the nerves,' I said.

"And then came Christmas. It was a German Christmas with German cakes and a tree for each of the boys. Gretchen and I had planned it one evening when Ruth was in bed with a headache.

"The gifts on our Christmas trees were magnificent. They were a surprise to me. Ruth and I had not believed in costly gifts, and now Ruth had loaded the trees with them. The trees were filled with toys, costly mechanical toys for each of our two boys. With them she had planned to win the boys.

"The boys were beside themselves with joy. They ran about

the room shouting. They played with the elaborate toys on the floor.

"Ruth took the gifts from the trees. In the shadow by the door stood Gretchen. She was silent. When the boys got the packages from the trees they ran to her, shouting, '*Mach' es auf! Mach' es auf! Tante Gretchen!'*

"I was happy. I thought we were having a beautiful Christmas. The annoyance I had felt at the magnificence of Ruth's gifts passed away.

"And then, in one moment, the struggle that had smouldered under the surface of the lives of the two women in my house burst forth. Ruth, my gentle Ruth, ran out into the middle of the floor, shouting in a shrill, high voice, 'Who is mother here? Whose children are these?'

"The two boys clung to the dress of Gretchen. They were frightened and cried. Gretchen went out of the room, taking them with her. I could hear her quick, firm footsteps on the stairs.

"Gretchen put the two boys into their white beds in the nursery. At her word they ceased weeping.

"In the center of the room they had left, lighted only by the little electric bulbs in the branches of the Christmas trees, stood Ruth. She stood in silence, looking at the floor, and trembling.

"I looked at the door through which our boys had gone at the command of Gretchen. I did not look at Ruth. A flame of indignation burned in me. I felt that I should like to take her by the shoulders and shake her."

Fordyce had never seen his friend so moved. Since his visit to Cottesbrooke he had been thinking of his old comrade as a man in a safe harbor—one peacefully becalmed behind the breakwater of Ruth and her fortune, passing his days untroubled, secure in his happiness.

"My Ruth is wonderful," declared Harkness, breaking in on these reflections. "She is all love and truth. To me she has been more dear than life. We have been married all these years, and still like a lover I dream of her at night. Sometimes I get out of bed and creep into her room, and, kneeling there in the darkness, I kiss the strands of her hair that lie loose upon the pillow.

"I do not understand why it is not with our boys as it is with me," he said, simply. "To myself I say, 'Her love should conquer all.'"

Before the mind of Fordyce was a different picture—the picture of a strong, straight-backed woman running down a gravel path to a wire rabbit-pen. He saw her reach through the door, and, taking the father rabbit by the ears, throw him through the window of the child's play-house. "She could settle the trouble in the rabbit's pen," he thought; "but this is another problem."

Harkness talked again. "I went to where Ruth stood trembling and took her in my arms," he said. "I made up my mind that I would send Gretchen back to Germany. It was my love for Ruth that had made my life. In a flash I saw how she had been crowded out of her place in her own home by that able, quiet, efficient woman."

Harkness turned his face away from the eyes of his friend. "She lay in my arms and I ran my hand over her hot little head," he said. 'I couldn't keep it back any longer, Joe; I couldn't help saying it,' she cried. 'I have been a child, and I have lost a fight. If you will let me, I will try now to be a woman and a mother.'"

Fordyce took his eyes from the face of his friend. For relief he had been feeding an old fancy. He saw himself walking up a gravel path to the door of a German house. The house would be in a village, and there would be formal flowerplots by the side of the gravel path.

"To what place in Germany did she go, this Gretchen?" he demanded.

Harkness shook his head. "She married Hans, the stableman, and they went away together," he said. "In my house the mechanical toys from the Christmas tree lie about underfoot. We are planning to send our boys to a private school. They are pretty hard to control."

39

Making the Farm Paper Alive for the Farm Woman

Agricultural Advertising 26 (August 1914): 43–44.

✒ *In all the* recent stir of things in the world there is nothing so interesting and significant as the movement of the women which is taking them into all forms of industrial and political life, and which will no doubt work a tremendous change in the affairs of the world. Woman's participation in the Government is almost accomplished, and woman's part in the business of the world is a fact already established.

For a long time I have been wondering why the farm papers are not devoting more space and taking a more active part in the distribution of knowledge regarding this movement of the women. They have their departments of Cookery and Dressmaking. Why not also their department devoted to the enlightenment of country women as to what is transpiring in a movement so interesting to them?

Agricultural Advertising is devoted to advertising and to merchandizing of goods. It does not pretend to discuss the right and wrong of the suffrage movement with all its influence on woman's work and thought.

But very much we are interested in the thing that will make the farm woman read the farm paper with greater interest. She buys most of the supplies for the house, and in a surprising number of cases has a word to say as to which shall be bought for the farm and the field.

I have recently spent some months in the country and have talked with a good many farm women on this subject. In the isolated farm houses women have many hours for thought and are curiously interested in what is going on among their sisters in the towns and cities. In every talk I had with farm women they were eager for discussion of woman's probable future place in the world.

Why not a department devoted to the matter in every farm paper? Why not more attention to a movement that is concerning all women? In a surprising number of cases the farm paper is the only publication that goes into the home of the farmer, and we believe that a department devoted to women's movements would be eagerly read by the women of the house.

The farmer's wife doesn't play bridge and she doesn't dance the tango. Hers is a serious, hard working business, and when she begins to vote she will vote seriously.

The farm paper that begins to help the farmer's wife now by interesting and enlightening her on the subject in which she is so much interested will win a place in her regard that it will not lose when she begins to make, as well as to mother, Presidents and Governors.

Incidentally, in making the farm paper that much more interesting to the woman of the farm, the publisher will be helping every advertiser who wants to appeal with his copy to the woman.

After this final contribution to Agricultural Advertising, *Sherwood Anderson did not publish any more stories or essays for fifteen months—until the end of 1915. Occupied with a new woman to love, Tennessee Mitchell, a free-spirited member of the Chicago Renaissance artistic group, a woman who was at one time involved with Edgar Lee Masters, the Chicago lawyer and poet whose* Spoon River Anthology *appeared to shocked acclaim in 1915, Tennessee and Sherwood in their relationship maintained separate lives and allowed each other the personal freedom believed in if seldom practiced successfully by their circle of advanced-thinking friends.*

By the autumn of 1914, Sherwood Anderson had taken for lodgings in Chicago an upper chamber in a rooming house at 735 North Cass Street (now Wabash Avenue). Again, as in his attic study in Elyria, Ohio, where he had first begun writing novels in time taken from his businesses, he found in a simple room the privacy and the intensity of concentration that allowed him to struggle with his fiction. Giving his first priority to making publishable at least two of the drafted Elyria novels, Anderson for self-reassurance wrote in 1915 and 1916 several sketches and stories that declared and confirmed his faith in his chosen true profession of creative writing. For his third contribution to Margaret Anderson's Little Review, *Anderson wrote this allegorical discussion of the artist and his inspiration.*

40

Sister

Little Review 2 (December 1915): 3–4.

❧ *The young artist* is a woman, and at evening she comes to talk to me in my room. She is my sister, but long ago she has forgotten that and I have forgotten.

Neither my sister nor I live in our father's house, and among all my brothers and sisters I am conscious only of her. The others have positions in the city and in the evening go home to the house where my sister and I once lived. My father is old and his hands tremble. He is not concerned about me, but my sister who lives alone in a room in a house on North Dearborn Street has caused him much unhappiness.

Into my room in the evening comes my sister and sits upon a low couch by the door. She sits cross-legged and smokes cigarettes. When she comes it is always the same—she is embarrassed and I am embarrassed. When she was quite young she was awkward and boyish and tore her clothes climbing trees. It was after that her strangeness began to be noticed. Day after day she would slip away from the house and go to walk in the streets. She became a devout student and made such rapid strides in her classes that my mother—who to tell the truth is fat and uninteresting—spent the days worrying. My sister, she declared, would end by having brain fever.

When my sister was fifteen years old she announced to the family that she was about to take a lover. I was away from home at the time, on one of the wandering trips that have always been a passion with me.

My sister came into the house, where the family were seated at the table, and, standing by the door, said she had decided to spend the night with a boy of sixteen who was the son of a neighbor.

The neighbor boy knew nothing of my sister's intentions. He was at home from college, a tall, quiet, blue-eyed fellow, with his mind set upon foot-ball. To my family my sister explained that she would go to the boy and tell him of her desires. Her eyes flashed and she stamped with her foot upon the floor.

My father whipped my sister. Taking her by the arm he led her into the stable at the back of the house. He whipped her with a long black whip that always stood upright in the whip-socket of the carriage in which, on Sundays, my mother and father drove about the streets of our suburb. After the whipping my father was ill.

I am wondering how I know so intimately all the details of the whipping of my sister. Neither my father nor my sister have told me of it. Perhaps sometime, as I sat dreaming in a chair, my mother gossiped of the whipping. It would be like her to do that, and it is a trick of my mind never to remember her figure in connection with the things she has told me.

After the whipping in the stable my sister was quite changed. The family sat tense and quiet at the table and when she came into the house she laughed and went upstairs to her own room. She was very quiet and well-behaved for several years and when she was twenty-one inherited some money and went to live alone in the house on North Dearborn Street. I have a feeling that the walls of our house told me the story of the whipping. I could never live in the house afterwards and came away at once to this room where I am now and where my sister comes to visit me.

And so there is my sister in my room and we are embarrassed. I do not look at her but turn my back and begin writing furiously. Presently she is on the arm of my chair with her arm about my neck.

I am the world and my sister is the young artist in the world. I am afraid the world will destroy her. So furious is my love of her that the touch of her hand makes me tremble.

My sister would not write as I am now writing. How strange it would be to see her engaged in anything of the kind. She would never give the slightest bit of advice to anyone. If you were dying and her advice would save you she would say nothing.

My sister is the most wonderful artist in the world, but when she is with me I do not remember that. When she has talked of her adventures, up from the chair I spring and go ranting about the room. I am half blind with anger, thinking perhaps that strange, furtive looking youth, with whom I saw her walking yesterday in the streets, has had her in his arms. The flesh of my sister is sacred to me. If anything were to happen to her body I think I should kill myself in sheer madness.

In the evening after my sister is gone I do not try to work any more. I pull my couch to the opening by the window and lie down. It is then a little that I begin to understand my sister. She is the artist right to adventure in the world, to be destroyed in the adventure, if that be necessary, and I, on my couch, am the worker in the world, blinking up at the stars that can be seen from my window when my couch is properly arranged.

Absent from Anderson's 1915–16 allegories of artist and art is any sufficient expression of the immensity of his creative experience while living and writing in his room at 735 North Cass Street in Chicago. One winter night, Anderson came home from unsatisfying work in his advertising office and, baffled at making literature from the drafted novels carried from Ohio and worked on for months and months, he sat and quickly wrote through, with little substantial revision, a short story with mini-

mum plot, a sketch really, called "Hands," the imaginative construct of an infinitely lonely, sexually frustrated, and desperately unfulfilled, unimportant man living near an imaginary town called "Winesburg, Ohio."

Having failed at equalling any chosen models of realistic novel-writing, Anderson, thus, scarcely with thought, suddenly had taught himself to write from his imagination simply and sparely and yet truthfully—to make the luminous "moment" in a figure's life the center of character revelation in short fiction. The inspiration that led to this first of the Winesburg stories led Anderson to complete several more of the psychologically penetrating and narratologically innovative tales in the winter of 1916, while he concurrently wrote more analogical explorations of writer and subject matter, as in this story, published in the lively and entertaining New York magazine Smart Set, edited by H. L. Mencken and George Jean Nathan.

41

The Story Writers

Smart Set 48 (January 1916): 243–48.

❧ *Albert Prindle was* a young lawyer with a soul. He had a wife who sang in the church choir and was very neat and precise in her housekeeping. Prindle was a man who liked a certain disorder about him; "atmosphere" he called it. His wife, Doris Prindle, regarded all disorder as something approaching vice, and insisted, with a quiet firmness that did not encourage argument, that he keep his cigar ashes out of the flower pots and his pipe heels out of the dessert dishes. As Doris Prindle did the housework, made the dresses for their two little girls, did the family washing and even managed, out of their limited income, to put money in the bank, Prindle did not feel that he was in a position to protest.

At the same time he felt that there were things to be said for his point of view. He aspired to be a story writer, an artist leaving behind an undying name as well as a lawyer specializing in the collection of slow accounts. He had already written one story that was months coming back from a popular magazine, from which he argued that the editors of the magazine must surely have hesitated a long time before sending it back. Later he sent the same story to several other magazines whose editors returned it promptly enough, but then, he told himself, they were editors of second-rate magazines anyway and at best had not daring enough to publish the work of a new man.

Prindle felt that if he could get into the right atmosphere he could do some big work. On lazy summer afternoons he sat in his office filled with envy of those writers who had spent years in the Far West or in the frozen North or who, like Kipling, had put in their apprenticeship at the writer's trade in India, where adventure stalked through the hot tropic nights. When he read in a magazine of a well-known writer who had started through the South Seas in an open boat he walked up and down the rug in the narrow office muttering. "Of course," he said, "going where the air is heavy with romance and mystery. That's just what makes a writing man. You just give me that chance. Give me a few months in an atmosphere of adventure and of free, full living and I will make them look up: I wish I might have some such chance for real expression before I die."

Seeking atmosphere Prindle had tried the experiment of arranging a room in the attic of his home for what he called a "workshop." He adorned the walls of the room with prints cut from magazines and had in it a writing desk he had made after a plan shown in an arts and crafts publication. For an hour or two after dinner Prindle wrote religiously all through one winter until one wet evening when he came home to find the family washing strung up in his "workshop." After that he felt that the place had in some way lost a certain flavor he had been trying very hard to give it.

This flavor Prindle could never quite achieve in his own house. Things were always happening. When he had got into the evening's work—"the sweat of composition," he loved secretly to call it—the younger daughter, in the nursery below, was likely to begin demanding a drink of water. Just when the scheming old political boss, in league with the interests, had left the papers lying on the window sill where the mischievous raven could snatch them and carry them to the office of the brilliant young reformer, intent upon breaking up the courthouse ring, a voice would come floating up to him from the livingroom. "Albert, will you get Esther a drink?" the voice would ask. "I have a headache." A man can't get back into a story after that.

And so Prindle started out to find his atmosphere. Out into the streets he went in the evening and strolled thoughtfully along trying to find a way out of his difficulty. "I need the exercise," he told Doris, who he felt wouldn't understand. Walking through the quiet streets he dreamed of fortunes coming to him from mysterious uncles or from grateful old ladies to whom he had given a seat in the street car, fortunes with which he could live the free open life of his dreams. He should have liked a year in Europe or in some wild land of adventure but in the end decided that the hostages he had given to fortune made these things impossible.

Prindle stood one evening under the awning by Appleby's grocery store on Thirty-third Street thinking of all these things when Appleby came out and joined him. The two men stood in friendly talk. On an impulse Prindle told Appleby what was in his mind. He felt that he had to talk to someone about it. To his surprise he found that Appleby also nursed in his apron-covered bosom a love of the art of words. He invited Prindle into the store and, taking a manuscript out of a coat hanging on a nail by the icebox, began reading to him a tale on which at odd moments he had been working. "Of course, " he said, "it needs working over."

Prindle leaned over the counter and scratched his head. "You have got them in a rather bad hole," he said judiciously. "What are you going to make them do now? How are you going to get them out of the mess?"

"That's just it," said Appleby. "It wants work there. I admit that. A fellow gets no time to think and work in a place like this. He is always having to stop to sell stuff. I think, of course, that the dark-eyed woman should die. I thought of letting her be killed in a railroad wreck or of making her take poison. The trouble is, Prindle, that I've never seen a railroad wreck nor a lady who has taken poison. I saw a man once who had delirium tremens in a restaurant, but that won't do me any good here. To tell the truth, I've never seen anything. I've had to stay right here selling soap and ham to support my family. I don't just know how to go at it to make it real. I think a man should stay true to life in a thing like this, don't you, Prindle?"

And so the two men had talked things over thoroughly. They decided that together they could afford to rent a room as a lodging for their two muses. Appleby had a cousin who was agent for a building on Fourth Street, and he thought that through him they could get something they could use at reduced rates. They really wanted a room with an open fire. Prindle thought that an open fire suggested stories and that they should have also a view of trees or of a running stream. Appleby agreed with him, but suggested that it would be as well to have the place where a man could drop in at odd moments as inspiration seized him. "We can give it a kind of Bohemian air," he said.

"'A la Bohème,' eh!" agreed Prindle, and left the hiring of the room in charge of the groceryman. He wondered if Appleby understood French.

For the next week the two men spent their evenings getting the room on Fourth Street fitted up. Prindle brought the prints from the walls of the deserted attic workshop. Failing an open fireplace, Appleby had picked up, at bargain figures, a small iron coal stove from a weeping old woman on Fourteenth Street. She was a scrub woman and explained to Appleby that she wanted the money to get her daughter out of trouble.

The girl had stolen a bolt of silk from a shop on Front Street and had been caught in the act by the store detective. She had always been a good girl, the mother explained, and had been kept in school only by great sacrifice on the mother's part. But she was inordinately fond of beautiful clothes and in a moment of weakness had gone into the store and stolen the silk for a new dress. "I had to stand listening to all that drivel," said Appleby, "but it was worth it, as I got a bargain on the stove."

Prindle brought in a box of little wooden figures and spread them out on the table. They had been carved by a half-witted boy who had taken them, as a gift, to a very beautiful girl, the daughter of a brewer. The brewer's family had reaped much fun out of the things, chaffing the girl on the havoc she worked in the hearts of the simple. Prindle had bought the figures at a bargain from the jeweler's son, a rosy-cheeked boy just growing into manhood, who had started dissipating secretly. He had read somewhere that a certain great dramatist used miniature figures of men and women, pushing them here and there on his study-table as he developed his plots.

The idea struck him as being a particularly good one. "That boy tried to gouge me. He wanted to tell me a long story about the number of years it took the half-witted boy to whittle the things out and how well they were done," said Prindle, "but I cut him short. I told him that I could buy what I wanted in a toy shop at five cents apiece and that's what I paid him."

There was some difference of opinion between the two men as to whether it would be better to have in the room one large table at which they could both work or two smaller tables at which, as Appleby said, each man could develop his own individuality. They settled on a long table with a row of dictionaries and standard classics to divide the two working ends.

On a Friday evening the room was ready. Appleby went over late in the afternoon and started a fire. On the way back to the store he smiled reflectively. "We've caught the atmosphere of art," he muttered, "there's some good work going to come out of that shop."

At eight o'clock Prindle got off the car at Appleby's store and the two men set out.

It was an early hour for closing Appleby's grocery store, but

Appleby felt that he had come to a moment when the ordinary course of events should be disregarded. The boy who usually closed the store had gone home to sit with a brother who was dying of tuberculosis. Appleby explained the case to Prindle as they walked along the street.

The Grady boy, he said, was a good boy. He had given up his chance for a college education and a career as a physician, on which his heart had been set, to help make comfortable the last days of an elder brother. The elder brother had been a newspaper reporter and had spoiled his career by an affair with a woman in a questionable resort. After a period of wild dissipation he had been stricken with tuberculosis and sending him to Colorado had exhausted the resources of the family. After all, as Appleby pointed out, the case had been hopeless from the first, and the money might have been saved. A complication of diseases had taken hold of the wasted body and the boy had been brought home and was patiently waiting for death. Appleby had been letting the Grady boy off early in the evening that he might help take care of the invalid. "I am sorry for the boy," he explained to Prindle, "but I am out of patience with the humdrum commonplaceness of such lives. I wish I might associate with men and women who really taste life, you know, the fellows that really get into the stream of things and see the romance of life flow past."

Prindle agreed with Appleby. "A nice mood I'm in for story writing this night of all nights," he cried impatiently. He explained that it had been a trying day at the office. A woman had come to him that afternoon—she was the widow of a fellow lawyer—and had spent the late afternoon telling him a tale of family unhappiness. She was a dull, uninteresting little woman who wanted to stay at home and bring up her family in a conventional, God-fearing way, who, by a streak of ill fortune, had married an indolent, imaginative, furiously jealous fellow who had wrecked their two lives. The woman had insisted on telling the intimate details of her unhappiness, and it had got Prindle's mind off his plot. "It was a flat affair, but it got on my nerves," he told Appleby. "You see, she met an old schoolfellow on the street and went to lunch with him. Her husband saw them going into the hotel. He had been drinking and followed them in and shot himself in their presence there in the dining room filled with people. Now his people are trying to keep her out of a share in her husband's fortune.

"By George, I'd like to meet one of the other kind of women, one of the dashing, daring, romantic kind," cried Prindle. "I'd like to have the young reformer in my story meet and be tempted by a real woman, a diamond thief or a spy for some foreign government.

As they climbed the stairs to the room on the fourth floor Prindle and Appleby came upon a pretty young girl who stood on the first landing with her lover. He was a young mechanic in his overalls, and with a very straight, manly body. From the darkness of the apartment in which the girl lived the voice of an old woman floated out to them. As they passed up a face appeared in the semi-darkness at the door. It was the face of an old woman with an evil, hard-looking mouth, and she was calling the pretty girl a hussy and demanding that the girl come into the house and wash the dishes.

On the fourth floor, in a room directly across from their new studio, lived an old man. He came out onto the landing as they climbed the stairs and after eyeing them suspiciously began locking his door. It was an elaborate locking. There was first the lock on the door itself, then two heavy padlocks passed through heavy staples and going on to both the top and bottom of the door. Finally there was a heavy iron bar that swung across the center of the door and locked into place.

Appleby explained to Prindle that the old man had been a successful contractor but had got half insane notions in his head. The real-estate cousin had gone into details about him. He was working on the model of a machine for recording thought. It was to be carried in his pocket and would record the thoughts of another person similarly equipped though the other person be thousands of miles away over mountain lake and forest.

Appleby and Prindle stood on the landing by their door discussing the old man who stood on the stairs watching them, his eyes filled with distrust. "He has been on the point of perfecting the foolish thing for the last five years," said Appleby, "and lives in fear that someone will steal his secret."

Appleby looked through a window to the street below. On a corner two young men were fighting furiously. A policeman coming up, they ran off down the street. Against a building stood a girl with a white, set face staring down the street after the running figures. "I might have the dark-eyed woman fall off a roof," he mused. "Now if there were only some natural way to get her up there." "It don't do to put anything gruesome into a story," said Prindle. "These editors are mighty ticklish about things like that."

In their room the two men stirred up the fire, although the night was mild, and got out their manuscripts preparatory to their evening's labor. They thought that the glowing stove would add atmosphere to the rather gloomy room. After a moment the stove made the room overwarm. They opened the window, but the roar of the street coming up disconcerted them. From the room below there came the sound of pounding and grinding. "It's a regular bedlam," complained Prindle. "If we're going to do any real work here we'll have to put a stop to that racket." They decided to investigate.

The occupant of the room below proved to be a blind man who supported himself and his daughter by grinding kitchen knives which the daughter collected and delivered during the day. He sat on a chair facing a grindstone, which was being turned by a slender, black-haired girl. He told the two men that he had been a fireman at a brick kiln in the hills back of the city and had been so cunning at keeping his fires alight and his wood for firing cut and ready that crowds of men and women sometimes came out of the city on Sunday afternoons to see the wonder of the blind man at his work. One night there had been a fire in the woods in the hills and the blind man told how he had made his way with difficulty through the roaring flames to a little creek at the foot of the hills and had waded down this to safety. The terrible experience had all but lost him the use of one of his legs and had forced him to take up a new occupation. He proved to be very reasonable and put off the grinding until later in the night, at the request of the storywriters.

Prindle and Appleby climbed the stairs again. They were nearly out of patience with the constant distracting adventures of the night. Silently they wrote for ten minutes and then there came a knocking at the door. Prindle got up and opened the door impatiently. A young Jewish boy came in and introduced himself. He had been told that they were writers and came to inquire if they took pupils and if their charges were high. He had come out from Russia and had a sister who had been caught by the police at a revolutionist meeting and sent to Siberia. He was working in the warehouse of a wholesale grocery company and thought that if he could learn to write English he might get a chance as shipping clerk at a higher wage. He planned to save money with which to bribe the police and get his sister to America.

Appleby was in a temper. He dismissed the boy with brutal levity. "This place will never do for us," he cried, "the greatest genius on earth couldn't work out stories in a hubbub like this."

Prindle, looking up sadly, shook his head. The two men went back to their places at the long table and for ten minutes bent silently over their work.

"Do you think that a story should be started with a quotation, you know, a line or two from some famous poem?" asked Appleby. Prindle had noticed that some of the other great writers did that.

There came a medley of shouts and oaths from the street below. The two men ran to the open window. A tiny girl, hurrying across the street from a corner saloon with a foaming pitcher of beer, had been run down by a speeding motorcyclist. She was apparently not seriously hurt and the two men saw her standing in the gutter sobbing and holding in her hand the handle of the broken pitcher. The rider, jumping on his machine, was trying to escape. Men ran shouting and swearing out of stores. A mountain of a man jumped from a passing car and, grabbing the fleeing rider by the collar, shook him until his coat came off and he fell to the pavement. Jerking the fallen man to his feet again, the huge fellow shook until the trousers, the seat of which he had clutched, were torn to the knees. Clutching again, the big man shook the now limp rider until, with a loud, tearing sound, the shirt came away from his back in two long strips. The rider ran down the middle of the street, holding up his torn trousers. The crowd jeered and shouted with delight. The huge man took the motorcycle and very deliberately pounded it into scrap iron against a telephone pole.

Appleby and Prindle, grabbing their hats, ran hurriedly down the stairs. They stood on the sidewalk and waved their hands joyously over the destruction of the machine. Under the lamplight Prindle recognized the large man as a famous jurist from the federal bench. They decided to give up writing for the evening and as they walked home together they talked again of their work.

"If I only knew just how to describe a railroad wreck," said Appleby, "if I had ever seen a wreck, I could make a real story out of that start of mine. A woman, such as I have drawn there, would never give up her grip on a man. She should die for the good of the story, but she should die in a big, smashing way."

"That's the trouble with men like you and me trying to write," said Prindle. "We don't have a chance to see the big things, the romance, of life. The big, primitive emotions never come to the men and women we see and know. Sometimes I think I'll quit trying. Nothing will ever happen to me, I know just how it will be. Everything will just go on forever flat and stale. The dead level of life—that's what I call [it]—the atmosphere we live in."

For his fourth contribution to the Little Review, *Anderson created an essay about his conception of how writing gets written, an account of inspiration that draws together his belief in the close alliance of human love and artistic creation. Most interesting aspect of this essay is the likelihood that, in creating a sympathetic relationship of understanding and tolerance between the unworldly writer and his practical employer, Anderson is presenting an image of his own grateful dependency on the tolerant beneficence of his supervisor at the advertising agency where he yet had to labor at earning his living.*

42

The Novelist

Little Review 2 (January–February 1916): 12–14.

❦ *The novelist is* about to begin the writing of a novel. For a year he will be at the task and what a year he will have! He is going to write the story of Virginia Borden, daughter of Fan Borden, a Missouri River raftsman. There in his little room he sits, a small, hunched-up figure with a pencil in his hand. He has never learned to run a typewriter and so he will write the words slowly and painfully, one after another on the white paper.

What a multitude of words! For hours he will sit perfectly still, writing madly and throwing the sheets about. That is a happy time. The madness has possession of him. People will come in at the door and sit about, talking and laughing. Sometimes he jumps out of his chair and walks up and down. He lights and relights his pipe. Overcome with weariness he goes forth to walk. When he walks he carries a heavy walking stick and goes muttering along.

The novelist tries to shake off his madness but he does not succeed. In a store he buys cheap writing tablets and, sitting on a stone near where some men are building a house, begins again to write. He talks aloud and occasionally fingers a lock of hair that falls down over his eyes. He lets his pipe go out and relights it nervously.

Days pass. It is raining and again the novelist works in his room. After a long evening he throws all he has written away.

What is the secret of the madness of the writer? He is a small man and has a torn ear. A part of his ear has been carried away by the explosion of a gun. Above the ear there is a spot, as large as a child's hand, where no hair grows.

The novelist is a clerk in a store in Wabash Avenue in Chicago. When he was a quite young man he began to clerk in the store and for a time promised to be successful. He sold goods, and there was something in his smile that won its way into all hearts. How he liked the people who came into the store and how the people liked him!

In the store now the novelist does not promise to be successful. There is a kind of conspiracy in the store. Although he tries earnestly he continues to make mistakes and all of his fellows conspire to forgive and conceal his mistakes. Sometimes when he has muddled things badly they are impatient and the manager of the store, a huge, fat fellow with thin grey hair, takes him into a room and begins to scold.

The two men sit by a window and look down into Wabash Avenue. It is snowing and people hurry along with bowed heads. So much do the novelist and the fat grey-haired man like each other that the scolding does not last. They begin to talk and the hours pass. Presently it is time to close the store for the night and the two go down a flight of stairs to the street.

On the corner stands the novelist and the store-manager, still talking. Presently they go together to dine. The manager of the store looks at his watch and it is eight o'clock. He remembers a dinner engagement with his wife and hurries away. On the street car he blames himself for his carelessness. "I should not have tried to reprimand the fellow," he says, and laughs.

It is night and the novelist works in his room. The night is cold and he opens a window. There is, in his closet, a torn woolen jacket given him by a friend, and he wraps the jacket about him. It has stopped snowing and the stars are in the sky.

The talk with the store-manager has inflamed the mind of the novelist. Again he writes furiously. What he is now writing will not fit into the life-story of Virginia Borden but, for the moment, he thinks that it will and he is happy. Tomorrow he will throw all away, but that will not destroy his happiness.

Who is this Virginia Borden of whom the novelist writes and why does he write of her? He does not know that he will get money from his story and he is growing old. What a foolish affair. Presently there may be a new manager in the store and the novelist will lose his place. Once in a while he thinks of that and then he smiles.

The novelist is not to be won from his purpose. Virginia Borden is a woman who lived in Chicago. The novelist has seen and talked with her. Like the store-manager she forgot herself talking to him. She forgot the torn ear and the bald spot where no hair grew and the skin was snow white. To talk with the novelist was like talking aloud to herself. It was delightful. For a year she knew him and then went away to live with a brother in Colorado where she was thrown from a horse and killed.

When she lived in Chicago many people knew Virginia Borden. They saw her going here and there in the streets. Once she was married to a man who was leader of an orchestra in a theater but the marriage was not a success. Nothing that Virginia Borden did in the city was successful.

The novelist is to write the life story of Virginia Borden. As he begins the task a great humbleness comes over him. Tears come into his eyes. He is afraid and trembles.

In the woman who talked and talked with him the novelist has seen many strange, beautiful, unexpected little turns of mind. He knows that in Virginia Borden there was a spirit that, but for the muddle of life, might have become a great flame.

It is the dream of the novelist that he will make men understand the spirit of the woman they saw in the streets. He wants to tell the store-manager of her and the little wiry man who has a desk next to his own. In the Wabash Avenue store there is a woman who sits on a high stool with her back to the novelist. He wants to tell her of Virginia Borden, to make her see the reality of the woman who failed, to make all see that such a woman once lived and went about among the women of Chicago.

As the novelist writes events grow in his mind. His mind is forever active and he is continually making up stories about himself. As the Virginia Borden whom men saw was a caricature of the Virginia Borden who lived in the mind of the novelist, so he knows that he is himself but a shadow of something very real.

And so the novelist puts himself into the book. In the book he is a large, square-shouldered man with tiny eyes. He is one who came to Chicago from a village in Poland and was leader of an orchestra in a theater. As the orchestra leader the novelist married Virginia Borden and lived in a house with her.

You see the novelist wants to explain himself also. He is a lover and so vividly does he love that he has the courage to love even himself. And so it is the lover that sits writing and the madness of the writer is the madness of the lover. As he writes he is making love. Surely all can understand that!

"Vibrant Life," with its imagery of strong sexual vitality desperate for expression amid the presence of physical death, is comparable to Anderson's earlier story "The Rabbit-Pen," written for Harper's. *Here the image of the stallion with life-force hardly to be contained replaces the image of the buck rabbit with maleness that only the strongest female ego can tame and fulfill.*

43

Vibrant Life

Little Review 3 (March 1916): 10–11.

❧ *He was a* man of forty-five, vigorous and straight of body. About his jaws was a slight heaviness, but his eyes were quiet. In his young manhood he had been involved in a scandal that had made him a marked man in the community. He had deserted his wife and children and had run away with a serious, dark-skinned young girl, the daughter of a Methodist minister.

After a few years he had come back into the community and had opened a law office. The social ostracism set up against him and his wife had in reality turned out to their advantage. He had worked fiercely and the dark-skinned girl had worked fiercely. At forty-five he had risen to wealth and to a commanding position before the bar of his state, and his wife, now a surgeon, had a fast-growing reputation for ability.

It was night and he sat in a room with the dead body of his younger brother, who had gone the road he had traveled in his twenties. The brother, a huge, good-natured fellow, had been caught and shot in the home of a married woman.

In the room with the lawyer sat a woman. She was a nurse, in charge of the children of his second wife, a magnificent blonde creature with white teeth. They sat beside a table, spread with books and magazines.

The woman who sat with the lawyer in the room with the dead man was, like himself, flush with life. He remembered, with a start, that she had been introduced into the house by the boy who was dead. He began to couple them in his mind and talked about it.

"You were in love with him, eh?" he asked presently.

The woman said nothing. She sat under a lamp with her legs crossed. The lamplight fell upon her shapely shoulders.

The lawyer, getting out of his chair, walked up and down the room. He thought of his wife, the woman he loved, asleep upstairs, and of the price they had paid for their devotion to each other.

"It is barbarous, this old custom of sitting up with the dead," he said, and, going to another part of the house, returned with a bottle of wine and two glasses.

With the wine before them the lawyer and the woman sat looking at each other. They stared boldly into each other's eyes, each concerned with his own thoughts. A clock ticked loudly and the woman moved uneasily. By an open window the wind stirred a white curtain and tossed it back and forth above the coffin, black and ominous. He began thinking of the years of hard, unremittent labor and of the pleasures he had missed. Before his eyes danced visions of white-clad dinner tables, with men and bare-shouldered women sitting about. Again he walked up and down the room.

Upon the table lay a magazine, devoted to farm life, and upon the cover was a scene in a barn yard. A groom was leading a magnificent stallion out at the door of a red barn.

Pointing his finger at the picture, the lawyer began to talk. A new quality came into his voice. His hand played nervously up and down the table. There was a gentle swishing sound of the blown curtain across the top of the coffin.

"I saw one once when I was a boy," he said, pointing with his finger at the stallion.

He approached and stood over her.

"It was a wonderful sight," he said, looking down at her. "I have never forgotten it. The great animal was all life, vibrant, magnificent life. Its feet scarcely touched the ground.

"We are like that," he added, leaning over her. "The men of our family have that vibrant, conquering life in us."

The woman arose from the chair and moved toward the darkened corner where the coffin stood. He followed slowly. When they had gone thus across the room she put up her hand and plead with him.

"No, no!— Think! Remember!" she whispered.

With a low laugh he sprang at her. She dodged quickly. Both of them had become silent. Among the chairs and tables they went, swiftly, silently, the pursuer and the pursued.

Into a corner of the room she got, where she could no longer elude him. Near her sat the long coffin, its ends resting on black stands made for the purpose. They struggled, and then, as they stood breathless with hot startled faces, there was a crash, the sound of broken glass, and the dead body of his brother with its staring eyes rolled, from the fallen coffin, out upon the floor.

There is some possibility that Windy McPherson's Son, *one of the novels that Sherwood Anderson had written while a businessman in Elyria, Ohio, could have been published soon after the author's escape to Chicago in 1913 if the author had agreed to extensive revision. Yet, with understandable pride in his first inspiration, Anderson would have resisted any suggestion that his storytelling was inferior, at least until the prospect of unrevised publication proved ever more indistinct. Whatever happened, by the beginning of 1916, Anderson had revised his novel and was soliciting the literary aid of Floyd Dell, H. L. Mencken, and Theodore Dreiser in placing it with a publisher. Although Dell deserves the credit for convincing the John Lane Company to publish* Windy McPherson's Son, *Anderson wrote almost immediately an impressionistic appreciation of Theodore Dreiser as a ponderous force for good in American literature. This tribute to Dreiser is Anderson's first expression of recognition and gratitude to any other author of his own generation and, hence, one of the first indications of his having read, perhaps widely, in American fiction published from 1900 to 1916.*

44

Dreiser

Little Review 3 (April 1916): 5.

Heavy, heavy, hangs over thy head.
Fine, or superfine.[1]

&   *Theodore Dreiser is* old—he is very, very old. I do not know how many years he has lived, perhaps thirty, perhaps fifty, but he is very old. Something gray and bleak and hurtful that has been in the world almost forever is personified in him.

When Dreiser is gone we shall write books, many of them. In the books we write there will be all of the qualities Dreiser lacks. We shall have a sense of humor, and everyone knows Dreiser has no sense of humor. More than that we shall have grace, lightness of touch, dreams of beauty bursting through the husks of life.

Oh, we who follow him shall have many things that Dreiser does not have. That is a part of the wonder and the beauty of Dreiser, the things that others will have because of Dreiser.

When he was editor of *The Delineator*, Dreiser went one day, with a woman friend, to visit an orphans' asylum.[2] The woman told me the story of that afternoon in the big, gray building with Dreiser, heavy and lumpy and old, sitting on a platform and watching the children—the terrible children—all in their little uniforms, trooping in.

"The tears ran down his cheeks and he shook his head," the woman said. That is a good picture of Dreiser. He is old and he does not know what to do with life, so he just tells about it as he sees it, simply and honestly. The tears run down his cheeks and he shakes his head.

Heavy, heavy the feet of Theodore. How easy to pick his books to pieces, to laugh at him. Thump, thump, thump, here he comes, Dreiser, heavy and old.

The feet of Dreiser are making a path for us, the brutal heavy feet. They are tramping through the wilderness, making a path.

Presently the path will be a street, with great arches over-head and delicately carved spires piercing the sky. Along the street will run children, shouting "Look at me"—forgetting the heavy feet of Dreiser.

The men who follow Dreiser will have much to do. Their road is long. But because of Dreiser, we, in America, will never have to face the road through the wilderness, the road that Dreiser faced.

> *Heavy, heavy, hangs over thy head.*
> *Fine or superfine.*

1. In the children's game, the "victim" must choose from impending consequences, to the degree of "fine" or "superfine."
2. In 1907 Theodore Dreiser became editor of *The Delineator,* a fashion magazine published by the Butterick company to advance sales of Butterick clothing patterns. Dreiser left the company in 1910.

In "The Struggle," published in May 1916, in Little Review, *Sherwood Anderson first demonstrated his use of the sympathetic "grotesque" as an element in storytelling, along with the device of the story presented as told to him by a participant in the action. Anderson would thereafter use often and to great advantage the idea that through physically grotesque characters an author can present emotional or psychological truth almost mystically pure in understanding and insight.*

45

The Struggle
Little Review 3 (May 1916): 7–10.

❧ *The story came* to me from a woman, met on a train. The car was crowded, and I took the seat beside her. There was a man in the offing, who belonged with her—a slender, girlish figure of a man, in a heavy brown canvas coat such as teamsters wear in the winter. He moved up and down in the aisle of the car, wanting my place by the woman's side, but I did not know that at the time.

The woman had a heavy face and a thick nose. Something had happened to her. She had been struck a blow or had a fall. Nature could never have made a nose so broad and thick and ugly. She talked to me in very good English. I suspect now that she was temporarily weary of the man in the brown canvas coat, that she had traveled with him for days, perhaps weeks, and was glad of the chance to spend a few hours in the company of someone else.

Everyone knows the feeling of a crowded train in the middle of the night. We ran along through western Iowa and eastern Nebraska. It had rained for days and the fields were flooded. In the clear night the moon came out and the scene outside the car-window was strange and in an odd way very beautiful. You get the feeling: the black bare trees standing up in clusters as they do out in that country, the pools of water with the moon reflected and running quickly as it does when the train hurries along, the rattle of the car-trucks, the lights in isolated farm-houses, and occasionally the clustered lights of a town as the train rushed through it into the West.

The woman had just come out of war-ridden Poland, had got out of that stricken land with her husband by God knows what miracles of effort. She made me feel the war, that woman did, and she told me the tale that I want to tell you.

I don't remember the beginning of our talk, nor can I tell you of how the strangeness of my mood grew to match her mood, until the story she told became a part of the mystery of the still night outside the car-window and very pregnant with meaning to me.

There was a company of Polish refugees moving along a road in Poland in charge of a German. The German was a man of perhaps fifty, with a beard. As I got him, he was much such a man as might be professor of foreign languages in a college in our country, say at Des Moines, Iowa, or Springfield, Ohio. He would be sturdy and strong of body and given to the eating of rather rank foods, as such men are. Also he would be a fellow of books and in his thinking inclined toward the ranker philosophies. He was dragged into the war because he was a German, and had steeped his soul in the German philosophy of might. Faintly, I fancy, there was another notion in his head that kept bothering him, and so to serve his government with a whole heart he read books that would re-establish his feeling for the strong, terrible thing for which he fought. Because he was past fifty he was not on the battle-line, but was in charge of the refugees, taking them out of their destroyed village to a camp near a railroad where they could be fed.

The refugees were peasants, all except the woman in the American train with me and her mother, an old woman of sixty-five. They had been small land-owners and the others in their party were women who had worked on their estate. Then there was the one man, my companion's lover, weak in body and with bad eyes.

Along a country road in Poland went this party in charge of the German, who tramped heavily along, urging them forward. He was brutal in his insistence, and the old woman of sixty-five, who was a kind of leader of the refugees, was almost equally brutal in her constant refusal to go forward. In the rainy night she stopped in the muddy road and her party gathered about her. Like a stubborn old horse she shook her head and muttered Polish words. "I want to be let alone, that's what I want. All I want in the world is to be let alone," she said, over and over; and then the German came up, and putting his hand on her back pushed her along, so that their progress through the dismal night was a constant repetition of the stopping, her muttered words, and his pushing. They hated each other with whole-hearted hatred, that old Polish woman and the German.

The party came to a clump of trees on the bank of a shallow stream. The German took hold of the old woman's arm and dragged her through the stream while the others followed. Over and over she said the words: "I want to be let alone. All I want in the world is to be let alone."

In the clump of trees the German started a fire. With incredible efficiency he had it blazing high in a few minutes, taking the matches and even some bits of dry wood from a little rubber-lined pouch carried in his inside coat-pocket. Then he got out tobacco, and, sitting down on the protruding root of a tree, smoked, and stared at the refugees, clustered about the old woman on the opposite side of the fire.

The German went to sleep. That was what started his trouble. He slept for an hour, and when he awoke the refugees were gone. You can imagine him jumping up and tramping heavily back through the shallow stream and along the muddy road to gather his party together again. He would be angry through and through, but he would not be alarmed. It was only a matter, he knew, of going far enough back along the road, as one goes back along a road for strayed cattle.

And then, when the German came up to the party, he and the old woman began to fight. She stopped muttering the words about being let alone and sprang at him. One of her old hands gripped his beard and the other buried itself in the thick skin of his neck.

The struggle in the road lasted a long time. The German was tired and not as strong as he looked, and there was that faint thing in him that kept him from hitting the old woman with his fist. He took hold of her thin shoulders and pushed, and she pulled. The struggle was like a man trying to lift himself by his boot-straps. The two fought and were full of the determination that will not stop fighting, but they were not very strong physically.

And so their two souls began to struggle. The woman in the train made me understand that quite clearly, although it may be difficult to get the sense of it over to you. I had the night and the mystery of the moving train to help me. It was a physical thing, the fight of the two souls in the dim light of the rainy night on that deserted muddy road. The air was full of the struggle, and the refugees gathered about and stood shivering. They shivered with cold and weariness, of course, but also with something else. In the air, everywhere about them, they could feel the vague something going on. The woman said that she would gladly have given her life to have it stopped, or to have someone strike a light, and that her man felt the same way. It was like two winds struggling, she said, like a soft yielding cloud become hard and trying vainly to push another cloud out of the sky.

Then the struggle ended and the old woman and the German fell down exhausted in the road. The refugees gathered about and waited. They thought something more was going to happen, knew in fact something more would happen. The feeling they had persisted, you see, and they huddled together and perhaps whimpered a little.

What happened is the whole point of the story. The woman in the train explained it very clearly. She said that the two souls, after struggling, went back into the two bodies, but that the soul of the old woman went into the body of the German and the soul of the German into the body of the old woman.

After that, of course, everything was quite simple. The German sat down by the road and began shaking his head and saying he wanted to be let alone, declared that all he wanted in the world was to be let alone, and the Polish woman took papers out of his pocket and began driving her companions back along the road, driving them harshly and brutally along, and when they grew weary pushing them with her hands.

There was more of the story after that. The woman's lover, who had been a school-teacher, took the papers and got out of the country, taking his sweetheart with him. But my mind has forgotten the details. I only remember the German sitting by the road and muttering that he wanted to be let alone, and the old tired mother-in-Poland saying the harsh words and forcing her weary companions to march through the night back into their own country.

The last of Sherwood Anderson's writings that can properly be called "apprentice" work is an essay, in story form, on the fate of an idealistic artist who is forced to survive in a commercialized world. Published in the June 1916, issue of Forum, *"Blackfoot's Masterpiece" may be read as Anderson's impassioned defense of creativity that must support itself in—and be maltreated by—the world of dollars and cents, a world where there is only the cruel consumption of art without understanding of the emotional cost of art to the artist. Artistic integrity maintained at the expense of madness may, in the extreme case of this exemplary artist, be the ultimate and inevitable price to be paid by the eccentric, nonconforming artistic genius.*

46

Blackfoot's Masterpiece

Forum 55 (June 1916): 679–83.

❧ *I came out* of the Fifth Avenue Auction Room and it was snowing. I had just seen Blackfoot's canvas sold for twenty thousand dollars and Ramsey, the connoisseur and dealer, had come up to my friend Trycup, who stood fingering a stick beside me, and had made a little speech. Trycup, like Blackfoot before him, is a painter of promise. Blackfoot, you know, went insane, is tucked away in some asylum upstate. Ramsey touched Trycup on the shoulder and spoke benevolently. I couldn't stand it. The speech made me half ill. "Keep your shoulders straight, my boy," said Ramsey. "Breathe deeply and keep your shoulders straight."

I went over to Fifty-eighth Street and asked a woman to dine with me. She is a sensitive, aristocratic-looking woman, come from somewhere out in the Middle West, and I wanted to hurt her. I thought I should tell her the story and watch her sensitive face quiver. There was something almost perverse in my desire to hurt so lovely a child and there is some of the same perversion in my wanting to see Blackfoot's story spread upon the printed page. I want to hurt many people, if I can.

As I went into the restaurant with my woman friend that evening after the picture was sold, the proprietor stepped forward to take my coat. He is grey and unctuous and looks like Ramsey. His hand fell on my shoulder and I heard his voice saying softly, "You've become a bit round-shouldered, my boy. Better straighten up. Get into the habit of breathing deeply and throw your shoulders back."

I didn't hit the restaurant man. Perhaps my hand trembled too much. Instead I snatched the coat from his hands and ran and the woman ran after me. "You go to the devil," I shouted to the man and when the woman caught up to me I went along past droves of people, past the dead, perplexed, evil-looking people who let the great Blackfoot go insane in their midst, telling the tale I now tell to you. It hurt my woman friend as I knew it would. I hope it will hurt you also.

Blackfoot was a poor artist in New York City twenty years ago. That isn't anything special, but then you see he was a real artist and that is always something special. He was married to the daughter of a laundry-man and lived over in that medley of streets in lower Manhattan, known as Greenwich Village.

I won't talk of his poverty. It was horrible, but that isn't the point. Comfort and an established place in the world are sometimes quite as horrible. Anyway, there he was in the dark, cheap little flat, with children crawling about underfoot, and other children always coming, and disorder and dirt everywhere about him.

Blackfoot was a thin, pale man of thirty, and he was round shouldered. He should have straightened his shoulders and breathed more deeply, there can be no doubt of that. It is a good rule for any man to adopt who marries a laundry-man's daughter, given to the having of babies, and who lives with her in a flat in Greenwich Village in New York City.

One day Blackfoot painted this picture. He got to work at it one gloomy morning in February and something happened. Order sprang out of disorder. His brush fairly sang across the canvas. All day he worked and half the next day, and his soul was glad. He forgot all of the facts of his disorderly life and just worked. The picture had everything in it—balance, poise, movement, and that most damnably elusive of all things in a work of art, sheer lyrical beauty.

Of course, Blackfoot felt like quite a man when the job was done. He put on a frayed overcoat and hunted out a cane he hadn't carried for five years, and then he went striding off to see Ramsey. He knew Ramsey would know what he had done and that Ramsey had money. It is a combination hard to find. There wasn't anyone to go to but Ramsey, you see.

As Blackfoot went along he came to a resolution. The most absurd notion came to his mind. He put a price on the picture he had painted. "I'll have twelve hundred dollars for it, by God," he told himself.

Blackfoot met Fred Morris on the street. Everyone in New York knows Fred. He is a good soul who makes money out of art, and paints pictures that sell. He was genuinely interested in what Blackfoot had done and congratulated him. "Good work, old man," he said, when the excited artist had told him the story, and then he touched Blackfoot on the shoulder with his stick. "You want to straighten yourself up," he said. "You're getting a little too round-shouldered. I take a walk every after-noon and throw my shoulders back. It has been good for me. You had better do that."

Ramsey came the next morning to see Blackfoot's picture. You get a sense of him, grey and quiet and sure, picking his way through Blackfoot's place among the kids and into the room where the picture was hung. He knew at once that a big job had been done and frankly said so. "Of course," he said, "you have come through big. What do you want for the thing? I'll take it right now."

Blackfoot was glad. He knew what he had done, but he

wanted Ramsey to know also. "Twelve hundred dollars," he said quickly.

Ramsey shook his head. "I'll give a thousand," he answered, and when Blackfoot got angry and began to storm about the room, he was very gentlemanly and decent. "Let's let it go," he said. "It doesn't matter. No good our getting into a row. I think you are going to be a big man and frankly I don't want to quarrel with you." He started toward the door. "By George, Blackfoot, you have some fine children," he muttered. "Take good care of yourself. You have responsibility here. I've noticed you're getting a little round shouldered. I was in the army myself. That started me right. I got into the right physical habits, you see."

Blackfoot waited a week before he went back to Ramsey. In a way he thought he had been too hasty. "A man's got to take things as they come, and I can't expect to have others feel as I do about my work," he said. Putting on the frayed overcoat he went over to Ramsey's place, forgetting this time to carry the cane.

Ramsey showed his hoofs. He offered Blackfoot seven hundred dollars for the canvas. He was soft voiced and gentlemanly, just as before, but that's all he would give and Blackfoot just turned and went out through the door, too furious to speak. He wanted to kill someone. Artists are that way. When you apply what the world calls common sense business methods to your dealings with them, they don't understand.

Ramsey finally got the canvas for four hundred dollars. Blackfoot made two more trips to his place and the last time he gave up. He had come out of Ramsey's house and was standing in the grey twilight looking up and down the street, not intending to give in at all, and then he just did. Rushing back, he accepted the four hundred dollars for the canvas that later sold for twenty thousand, and took the money in bills on the spot.

I haven't, I hope, overdone Blackfoot's poverty. I don't really remember how many children he had, not more than three or four, perhaps, but there was another coming. Of course, he was in debt at the grocery and to the landlord and had no credit.

The four hundred helped a lot. Things were brought in and a woman was employed to clean up and feed the children. Blackfoot himself built a roaring fire in the fireplace in his wife's room. He seemed happy enough, but he was tired. At ten o'clock he went to bed in a room with two of the children.

That's the last anyone ever saw of Blackfoot. The chattering thing up in the asylum who runs about telling people to breathe deeply and straighten up their shoulders has nothing to do with the man who painted the canvas I saw sold today.

Blackfoot went out with a swing. Bless his heart for that. It must have been two o'clock in the morning when his wife awoke on her cot in the corner of the little living room, and saw her husband sitting in a chair by the open fire. He had on a torn pair of pajamas and one of the legs was ripped so that his long thin leg showed through, and the poor fool had searched out the walking stick and had it hanging on his arm. When his wife screamed he paid no attention at first, but presently he got up and came on tiptoe across the room to her. With the cane he touched her on the arm. "Straighten your shoulders," he said softly. "You must breathe deeply and throw your shoulders back."

That's all he said, and the wonder is that his wife did not go insane also. For when the woman awoke she saw something that must have made her heart stop beating. The thing she saw was as fine as the painting of the great picture. There in the firelight, in the little flat in Greenwich Village, with the cane hooked over his arm, Blackfoot had done a lovely thing. Alone in the silence, with his mind gone, and everyone asleep, he had fed the bills given him by Ramsey one by one into the fire.

&

Afterword

By the late summer of 1916, Sherwood Anderson finally had personal and professional reasons to be happy with his traumatic movement from Ohio businessman to Chicago writer. He had completed all work on *Windy McPherson's Son* and expected to receive copies of this first novel in the autumn, with his second novel, *Marching Men,* to be published in 1917. He had been divorced by Cornelia Lane Anderson and almost immediately become married to Tennessee Mitchell (a marriage that would last, at least legally, for over seven years). He had hope that he would eventually—perhaps soon—be able to abandon his work as an advertising writer and live on the income from his creative writing. And—above all else—he had written several superb stories about a young man named George Willard, the newspaper reporter in an imaginary Ohio town named Winesburg, where there lived also the beautifully presented "grotesques" whose lives Anderson had been inspired to begin creating in the winter of 1915–16 and whose stories, when presented in collected form in *Winesburg, Ohio* in the spring of 1919, would mark the artistic apogee of this Ohio businessman who had painfully and slowly reached his goal of literary artistry. The road from youthful, easy ambition to personal maturity and artistic achievement had been long and arduous; yet this early journey of enthusiastic adoption of a way of life and its subsequent rejection had set the configuration of the author's existence—a pattern that would continue to characterize Sherwood Anderson's life until his death in 1941.

Freed at last by 1922 of having to earn his living from the writing of advertisements in Chicago, Anderson became a wanderer across his nation, choosing to live for extended periods in New York City, in New Orleans, in San Francisco, in coastal Alabama, and—longest and last—in the mountains of the Virginia Highlands, and fortunate enough to travel to Europe three times; and yet, wherever he was and however content he might be with his surroundings, Anderson was almost constantly planning new journeys. Such continuous and extensive travels made Anderson, always a close observer of the life about him, one of the most effective social analysts of the American scene, his acute observations becoming most valuable as his nation entered and endured the Great Depression of the 1930s.

Only once did Anderson own a home—"Ripshin," in Southwest Virginia—and this home he used only in summer and often thought of selling. He was married two more times—in 1924 to Elizabeth Prall, well-educated and cultured daughter of a Michigan family; and finally in 1933 to Eleanor Copenhaver, committed social worker and daughter of one of the prominent families in Southwest Virginia. Only with Eleanor did Sherwood remain maritally content, for this last wife enjoyed and understood the rambling, never-satisfied life that her older husband enjoyed and needed.

It is as though Sherwood Anderson almost feared letting himself become settled and content with whatever activity and abode he took up, believing, perhaps subconsciously, that such rooted, fixed status threatened a return to the materialistic, conventional ambitions of his early manhood. He had had money once and he could, he knew, easily make money again, through writing advertisements or their equivalent in popular stories and novels; but such easy existence would defeat and kill the artist in him, and Anderson's inner artist required movement and scope and liberty from ordinary constraints of financial success and numbing social and residential stability.

Given the often unfulfilled literary ambitions that Anderson embraced and the more and more rare self-satisfaction and critical praise that he garnered from his novels and stories and essays and poems after the early 1920s, it must be stated firmly that, with the publication of *Winesburg, Ohio* (1919), *The Triumph of the Egg* (1921), and *Horses and Men* (1923), Sherwood Anderson truly was considered one of the leading authors of America—an author from whom even greater stories and novels might be expected. Yet in 1926 Anderson turned fifty and was unable to compete always happily and successfully with his own earlier achievements. He had become an influence on Ernest Hemingway and F. Scott Fitzgerald and William Faulkner; and as a literary influence he was already part of literary history while such younger authors as these were just ready to become the critical and cultural leaders of their own new (if "lost") literary generation.

Yet the many works of fiction and social observation that Sherwood Anderson wrote in the last two decades of his life are not to be ignored, for the road to artistry for this writer had been too difficult and too meaningful for him ever to become trivial or cheap or worthless in his writing: of all American writers, no one cared more about craft and faithfulness to that craft than did Anderson.

And the forty-six apprentice writings of Sherwood Anderson that constitute this book—from the essays on advertising in 1902 through the stories about the primacy of art and artist in 1916—all form a necessary introduction to the writings and the life that were to follow them, and those writings and that life document the fascinating passage of an important American author across the literary landscape of his nation.

A Note on Editing

My aim in republishing Sherwood Anderson's early essays and stories is to make these materials available, for the first time, in a convenient and useful volume. Therefore, I have very lightly edited the materials, when necessary, in order to provide the reader with consistent spelling, with orderly punctuation according to Anderson's habits, and with the words written by the author as unchanged as possible, consistent with conveying clear and easy understanding.

One problem of text encountered in preparing this volume requires some discussion. The pages of *Agricultural Advertising*, in which Anderson published most of his early essays, are replete with "filler"—short sentences or paragraphs of fact or opinion (seldom of real wit) placed at the ends of essays and poems and photographs and advertisements to complete the made-up pages of type. Previous examinations of issues of the periodical have led investigators to conclude that any such paragraphs appearing at the ends of Anderson's columns were necessarily written by Anderson himself and thus reflect his own ability at cleverness and sharpness.

I am unable to accept all of this "filler" as clearly Anderson's because, whenever Anderson's by-line comes at the close of his columns instead of at the beginning, the "filler" material *follows* his printed name and because the appearing material is often extracted from other periodicals and labeled as to source. Thus I have included in this book only the "filler" paragraphs that come at the ends of eight of Anderson's columns—material that might indeed have been written by him as part of his contributions to *Agricultural Advertising;* but the reader should remember that Anderson or the editors of the journal issues might silently have borrowed some of these paragraphs from available books of such "filler." It is important to note that these appended paragraphs appeared in Anderson's essays only from January through November 1903—that, as Anderson continued to write for publication and as he became more confident with his writing, he ceased to produce such material or to have such material printed with his essays, relying instead on his developing sense of rhetorical effectiveness and wholeness.

Select Bibliography

I. By Sherwood Anderson

Complete Works of Sherwood Anderson. Edited by Kichinosuke Ohashi. 21 volumes. Kyoto: Rinsen, 1982.

Windy McPherson's Son. New York: John Lane, 1916.

Marching Men. New York: John Lane, 1917.

Mid-American Chants. New York: John Lane, 1918.

Winesburg, Ohio. New York: B. W. Huebsch, 1919.

Poor White. New York: B. W. Huebsch, 1920.

Triumph of the Egg. New York: B. W. Huebsch, 1921.

Many Marriages. New York: B. W. Huebsch, 1923.

Horses and Men. New York: B. W. Huebsch, 1923.

A Story Teller's Story. New York: B. W. Huebsch, 1924.

Dark Laughter. New York: Boni and Liveright, 1925.

The Modern Writer. San Francisco: Gelber, Lilienthal, 1925.

Sherwood Anderson's Notebook. New York: Boni and Liveright, 1926.

Tar: A Midwest Childhood. New York: Boni and Liveright, 1926.

A New Testament. New York: Boni and Liveright, 1927.

Hello Towns! New York: Horace Liveright, 1929.

Nearer the Grassroots and Elizabethton. San Francisco: Westgate Press, 1929.

Alice and The Lost Novel. London: Elkin Mathews and Marrot, 1929.

The American County Fair. New York: Random House, 1930.

Perhaps Women. New York: Horace Liveright, 1931.

Beyond Desire. New York: Liveright, 1932.

Death in the Woods. New York: Liveright, 1933.

No Swank. Philadelphia: Centaur Press, 1934.

Puzzled America. New York: Charles Scribner's Sons, 1935.

Kit Brandon. New York: Charles Scribner's Sons, 1936.

Plays: Winesburg and Others. New York: Charles Scribner's Sons, 1937.

A Writer's Conception of Realism. Olivet, Mich.: Olivet College, 1939.

Five Poems. San Mateo, Calif.: New York: Alliance, 1939.

Sherwood Anderson's Memoirs. New York: Harcourt, Brace, 1942.

The Sherwood Anderson Reader. Edited by Paul Rosenfeld. Boston: Houghton Mifflin, 1947.

The Portable Sherwood Anderson. Edited by Horace Gregory. New York: Viking Press, 1949.

Letters of Sherwood Anderson. Edited by Howard Mumford Jones and Walter B. Rideout. Boston: Little, Brown, 1953.

Sherwood Anderson: Short Stories. Edited by Maxwell Geismar. New York: Hill and Wang, 1962.

Return to Winesburg. Edited by Ray Lewis White. Chapel Hill: University of North Carolina Press, 1967.

Sherwood Anderson's Memoirs: A Critical Edition. Edited by Ray Lewis White. Chapel Hill: University of North Carolina Press, 1969.

A Story Teller's Story: A Critical Edition. Edited by Ray Lewis White. Cleveland: Press of Case Western Reserve University, 1969.

Tar: A Midwest Childhood—A Critical Edition. Edited by Ray Lewis White. Cleveland: Press of Case Western Reserve University, 1971.

The Buck Fever Papers. Edited by Welford Dunaway Taylor. Charlottesville: University Press of Virginia, 1971.

Sherwood Anderson / Gertrude Stein: Correspondence and Personal Essays. Edited by Ray Lewis White. Chapel Hill: University of North Carolina Press, 1972.

The "Writer's Book" by Sherwood Anderson: A Critical Edition. Edited by Martha Mulroy Curry. Metuchen, N.J.: Scarecrow Press, 1975.

France and Sherwood Anderson: Paris Notebook, 1921. Edited by Michael Fanning. Baton Rouge: Louisiana State University Press, 1976.

Sherwood Anderson: The Writer at His Craft. Edited by Jack Salzman, David D. Anderson, and Kichinosuke Ohashi. Mamaroneck, N.Y.: Paul P. Appel, 1979.

The Teller's Tales. Introduction by Frank Gado. Schenectady: Union College Press, 1983.

Sherwood Anderson: Selected Letters. Edited by Charles E. Modlin. Knoxville: University of Tennessee Press, 1984.

Letters to Bab: Sherwood Anderson to Marietta D. Finley, 1916–33. Edited by William A. Sutton. Urbana: University of Illinois Press, 1985.

The Sherwood Anderson Diaries, 1936–1941. Edited by Hilbert H. Campbell. Athens: University of Georgia Press, 1987.

II. About Sherwood Anderson

Appel, Paul P., ed. *Homage to Sherwood Anderson.* Mamaroneck, N.Y.: Paul P. Appel, 1970.

Anderson, David D., ed. *Critical Essays on Sherwood Anderson.* Boston: G. K. Hall, 1982.

_____. *Sherwood Anderson: An Introduction and Interpretation.* New York: Holt, Rinehart and Winston, 1967.

_____, ed. *Sherwood Anderson: Dimensions of His Literary Art.*

East Lansing: Michigan State University Press, 1976.

Bruyère, Claire. *Sherwood Anderson: L'Impuissance Créatrice.* Paris: Klincksieck, 1985.

Burbank, Rex. *Sherwood Anderson.* New York: Twayne Publishers, 1964.

Campbell, Hilbert H., and Charles E. Modlin, eds. *Sherwood Anderson: Centennial Studies.* Troy, N.Y.: Whitson, 1976.

Howe, Irving. *Sherwood Anderson.* New York: William Sloane, 1951.

Mouscher, Karen-Elisabeth. "Sherwood Anderson: The Early Advertising Years." Dissertation, Northwestern University, 1986.

Rideout, Walter B., ed. *Sherwood Anderson: A Collection of Critical Essays.* Englewood Cliffs, N.J.: Prentice-Hall, 1974.

Rogers, Douglas G. *Sherwood Anderson: A Selective, Annotated Bibliography.* Metuchen, N.J.: Scarecrow Press, 1976.

Sheehy, Eugene P., and Kenneth A. Lohf. *Sherwood Anderson: A Bibliography.* Los Gatos, Calif.: Talisman Press, 1960.

Schevill, James. *Sherwood Anderson: His Life and Work.* Denver: University of Denver Press, 1951.

Sutton, William A. *The Road to Winesburg: A Mosaic of the Imaginative Life of Sherwood Anderson.* Metuchen, N.J.: Scarecrow Press, 1972.

Taylor, Welford Dunaway. *Sherwood Anderson.* New York: Ungar, 1977.

Townsend, Kim. *Sherwood Anderson.* Boston: Houghton Mifflin, 1987.

Weber, Brom. *Sherwood Anderson.* Minneapolis: University of Minnesota Press, 1964.

White, Ray Lewis. *Sherwood Anderson: A Reference Guide.* Boston: G. K. Hall, 1977.

———, ed. *The Achievement of Sherwood Anderson: Essays in Criticism.* Chapel Hill: University of North Carolina Press, 1966.

Williams, Kenny J. *A Storyteller and a City: Sherwood Anderson's Chicago.* DeKalb: Northern Illinois University Press, 1988.

III. Background Readings

Berthoff, Warner. *The Ferment of Realism: American Literature, 1884–1919*. New York: Free Press, 1965.

Cochran, Thomas C. *Basic History of American Business*, 2d ed. Princeton: D. Van Nostrand, 1968.

Cramer, Dale. *Chicago Renaissance: The Literary Life in the Midwest, 1900–1930*. New York: Appleton-Century, 1966.

Duffey, Bernard. *The Chicago Renaissance in American Letters: A Critical History*. East Lansing: Michigan State University Press, 1956.

Lord, Walter. *The Good Years from 1900 to the First World War*. New York: Harper & Row, 1960.

Martin, Jay. *Harvests of Change: American Literature, 1865–1914*. Englewood Cliffs, N.J.: Prentice-Hall, 1967.

May, Henry F. *The End of American Innocence: A Study of the First Years of Our Own Time, 1912–1917*. Chicago: Quadrangle, 1959.

Presbrey, Frank. *The History and Development of Advertising*. Garden City: Doubleday, Doran, 1929.

Schlebecker, John T. *Whereby We Thrive: A History of American Farming, 1607–1972*. Ames: Iowa State University Press, 1975.

Smith, Henry Justin. *Chicago's Great Century: 1833–1933*. Chicago: Consolidated, 1933.

United States Department of Commerce, Bureau of the Census. *Historical Statistics of the United States: Colonial Times to 1957*. Washington, D.C.: Government Printing Office, 1957.

Williams, Kenny J. *In the City of Men: Another Story of Chicago*. Nashville: Townsend Press, 1974.